## *Making Love.*
# The Words Whispered Through Gabe Griffin's Brain.

He could honestly say he'd never done that with a woman. Sex, yes. But love? He wasn't capable of loving someone, so the matter was insignificant. He cast another look at Calli Thornton, and she reached across to brush crumbs from his shirt. Her every gesture was giving and caring.

And he was lying to her.

A heaviness swelled in his chest, and Gabe had to look away. One thought kept coming back to him, making him ache for Calli in a way he'd never thought possible.

*Will she forgive me when she learns the truth?*

For the first time in years, Gabe allowed himself to hope for the impossible.

Dear Reader,

Where do you read Silhouette Desire? Sitting in your favorite chair? How about standing in line at the market or swinging in the sunporch hammock? Or do you hold out the entire day, waiting for all your distractions to dissolve around you, only to open a Desire novel once you're in a relaxing bath or resting against your softest pillow…? Wherever you indulge in Silhouette Desire, we know you do so with anticipation, and that's why we bring you the absolute best in romance fiction.

This month, look forward to talented Jennifer Greene's *A Baby in His In-Box,* where a sexy tutor gives March's MAN OF THE MONTH private lessons on sudden fatherhood. And in the second adorable tale of Elizabeth Bevarly's BLAME IT ON BOB series, *Beauty and the Brain,* a lady discovers she's still starry-eyed over her secret high school crush. Next, Susan Crosby takes readers on The Great Wife Search in *Bride Candidate #9.*

And don't miss a single kiss delivered by these delectable men: a roguish rancher in Amy J. Fetzer's *The Unlikely Bodyguard;* the strong, silent corporate hunk in the latest book in the RIGHT BRIDE, WRONG GROOM series, *Switched at the Altar,* by Metsy Hingle; and Eileen Wilks's mouthwatering honorable Texas hero in *Just a Little Bit Pregnant.*

So, no matter *where* you read, I know *what* you'll be reading— all six of March's irresistible Silhouette Desire love stories!

Regards,

Melissa Senate

Melissa Senate
Senior Editor
Silhouette Desire

Please address questions and book requests to:
Silhouette Reader Service
U.S.: 3010 Walden Ave., P.O. Box 1325, Buffalo, NY 14269
Canadian: P.O. Box 609, Fort Erie, Ont. L2A 5X3

# AMY J. FETZER
## THE UNLIKELY BODYGUARD

**SILHOUETTE** *Desire*®

Published by Silhouette Books

**America's Publisher of Contemporary Romance**

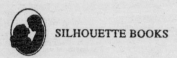

SILHOUETTE BOOKS

ISBN 0-373-76132-5

THE UNLIKELY BODYGUARD

This edition published by arrangement with Harlequin Books S.A.

® and TM are trademarks of Harlequin Books S.A., used under license.
Trademarks indicated with ® are registered in the United States Patent
and Trademark Office, the Canadian Trade Marks Office and in other
countries.

Printed in U.S.A.

**Books by Amy J. Fetzer**

Silhouette Desire

*Anybody's Dad* #1089
*The Unlikely Bodyguard* #1132

# AMY J. FETZER

was born in New England and raised all over the world. Married nineteen years to a United States Marine and the mother of two sons, Amy covets the moments when she can curl up with a cup of cappuccino and a good book.

To
Chef Sara E. Baker,
for all those delicious details about dangerous men
and
Darrell L. Mitchell
who has hero material written all over him,
even if he doesn't believe it.

# One

**E**very head in the joint turned when she stepped inside.

She hesitated, surveying the dim roadhouse, the neon glare of bar lights illuminating her from behind, leaving her face cast in shadows. Women spared her a glance. Men strained for a better look. Angel set his glass aside and stared. She walked slowly to the bar, the click of her heels marking the sultry shift of hips wrapped in a tight, black leather skirt. She had muscular legs up the kazoo and when she propped her elbows on the bar, her short leather jacket creaked.

From the description he had, he'd expected her to look like a schoolgirl. Not a centerfold. Black leather, tight and shaping her figure, told Angel and every man around exactly what was beneath. But even that body didn't compare to her face. A classic, pure beauty, he thought, like Snow White.

Hell. He'd had stranger fantasies.

She ordered a shot of tequila in a voice like rustling silk.

A mirror, dirty and cloudy from nicotine, ran the length of the wall and in it he watched her slide folded bills across the beer-splattered wood to the bartender. She picked up the shot and tossed it back. The glass came away from her mouth slowly, her tongue sliding across her lips. Abruptly, she turned the empty jigger rim down on the bar and ordered another. While the bartender poured, she took a step back, her hands braced as she stretched a bit. Several men lining the wood rail leaned back to inspect the shapely curve of her bottom and the black stockings seaming her incredible legs.

She didn't belong here. She stood out against the dingy bar like a baby in a wrestling ring. What did she hope to accomplish in The Rusty Nail?

Ike Granson, a petty thief and dealer, moved close to her, his voice too low to carry as he slid onto the stool beside hers. She tucked jaw-length black hair behind one ear, cocked her head to look at him and smiled. God, what a smile, Angel thought, and let his gaze discreetly follow her as she joined the man on the dance floor. The haze of smoke hovered around them like a filthy curtain. Ike bent, his oily hair spilling over his face as he whispered in her ear, his hand groping her spine like a lazy masseur. She stiffened and stopped, then she reared back and made a fist. Great.

Hail Mary, Calli thought. She was in trouble now. In over her head. Way in. She just *had* to go hunting for excitement, and as luck would have it, she'd picked the one club that promised a little *too much* local color. She'd never done anything quite this adventurous in her life and now that her first vacation in three years was swiftly going downhill, she wanted to just get away without getting her throat cut, or raped, or whatever. And not let anyone know how scared and stupid she felt. As casually as she could, she unfurled her fist.

"Ah, no thanks, pal. I'm not looking for that kind of company." *Not yours at least.* Ike smelled of pot, B.O. and booze. But he looked even worse. Greasy. And she'd had enough of being pawed. Stepping out from under his groping, she turned and walked back toward her seat at the bar. He caught her wrist, yanking her into his arms. Her hair spread over her face and he stroked it back. Yuk. Even his nails were dirty.

"You're out here showin' it off, slut, and I want some."

He pulled her flat against his bony body, arms tight around her, his hot, foul breath in her face and whispered what he really wanted to do with her.

Appalled, Calli asked, "Do you talk to your mother with that mouth?"

He scowled. "Don't be talkin' 'bout my mother."

*Careful,* a voice in her head warned, sounding too much like Sister Mary Elizabeth. "Look. What part of *no* don't you understand, so I can explain it?"

His face glowed with anger, his hold tightened. Uh-oh. Her mouth was going to get her into bigger trouble, she thought as she tried to peel his hands from her waist. She couldn't get a good grip. Fear stung up her spine. She kept telling herself she could get out of this. She could.

"I ain't never seen a woman turn you down that quick, Ike."

Ike's gaze slashed to an obese man lingering close. "And you ain't gonna."

His one hand drove lower, cupping her buttocks, and Calli's stomach pitched.

"I got a car out back. I can do ya quick."

She struggled. "Your charm amazes me. Ike, is it?" He grew ruder, and since he wasn't getting the message, she smacked his cheek, hard. His hiss of pain sounded loud in the suddenly quiet bar. She could feel people staring, yet he didn't release her. Instead, he smiled. Good Lord, he liked it, she realized, shoving at his chest. When that didn't dislodge him, she resorted to the only thing possible in this situation. She ground her four-inch stiletto heel down on his instep. He howled like a coyote and let her go.

So much for five years of karate, Calli thought, tugging at the hem of her jacket. "Now do you understand *no?*"

But his friend, the rudest-looking man in the free world, decided it was his turn and pushed his huge self off the bar stool. The motion spread open his leather vest and Calli was surprised to see that his nipples were tattooed like eyeballs.

"Good God. Did that hurt?" she asked, wide-eyed, then composed herself. "Of course it did." She met his muddy gaze. "It's not very attractive, you know."

He had arms like ham shanks and she should shut up, she knew. Ike was still soothing his foot, his eyes threatening retaliation, and Calli decided that an excellent time to leave was five minutes ago.

"I, ah, I've got to go," she said in a rush, easing back toward the door with tiny steps. "Ah—thanks for the dance," she said, peering around the fat man at Ike. The sisters of St. Andrew's Orphanage had insisted that saying please and thank you would always get one further than one thought. The good sisters needed a reality check, she decided.

"You're not leavin', little girl," he threatened, advancing on her. Calli's wide gaze shot between the two men. She instantly weighed her options, and a knee to the groin in the hope that his descendants would come out his throat was not one of them. And with his mammoth arms, any victory she could manage would last about two seconds.

"I really must," she said to his beefy chest, and hated the tremor in her voice. Hated the fear beginning to settle in the pit of her stomach. When he raised his hand to grab or strike her, Calli back-stepped faster and right into an unyielding body.

Just as quickly, a palm closed heavily over her left shoulder. Good God, she was surrounded. The fat man stopped, mid-grasp. Calli struggled under her captor's grasp, but she couldn't move, as if the hand was pushing her down into the concrete floor. *I'm toast.* She obeyed the silent command to be still, suppressing the fear singing through her body as the fat man's gaze shot to somewhere behind her.

High behind her.

And the angry flush in his face drained white.

"Leave her alone, Tiny." The voice was whiskey-rough and low. Undeniably sexy.

"She had it comin', Angel."

There was a stretch of silence before The Voice said, "Try again."

The unspoken threat hung in the dirty air.

Tiny's lips thinned, his eyes narrowing to slits.

"Step away from her."

Tiny obeyed, moving back a bit.

Very carefully, Calli turned her head and stared straight at a throat ringed by the collar of a dark T-shirt. She let her gaze climb, up the stubbled jaw and past the most incredible lips to a pair of frosty, mint-green eyes. He has the longest lashes, she thought absently. And a pierced ear. She wet her lips. *This* was Angel? He looked anything but. Tanned skin. Dark hair. Too pale eyes. He was danger. *Real* danger. There wasn't a sound in the bar except the jukebox and Calli shivered. Angel kept his gaze on Tiny, even though she knew he was aware of her stare. Calli couldn't remember seeing him when she came in. Hard to believe she'd missed him. But she didn't need rescuing.

"Back off, Angel."

His gaze slid to hers and Calli felt a jolt of primal sexuality shoot down her body to her pumps. He arched a brow, sinister, like a wing lifting for flight. "You *want* to go with him?"

God, that voice. She glanced at Tiny. "No."

"Then I suggest you shut up."

Her eyes widened. "Excuse me?"

"You ain't takin' her," Tiny found the nerve to say.

The liquor warming her veins made her bold. "And neither are you." She took advantage of his surprise and ducked under Angel's hold, slipped between the two men and walked back to the bar. *Go! Leave now!* a righteous voice screamed in her head. Instead, she fished in her purse, then slapped money on the counter to keep her hands from shaking. The bartender sloshed another shot into her glass, smirking to himself. In the mirror, she noticed that Tiny and Angel were still staring each other down like two gunfighters.

Finally, Tiny backed off, walked to a booth and slid his big body behind the table, next to Ike.

Angel turned his head to look at her. She met his gaze in the mirror, her drink stilling halfway to her lips. She felt like a fly caught in amber. Even from across the room it hurt to look into those eyes. A raw, hot feeling scrambled through her and the most erotic images came to mind. Then she blinked and shrugged away the playground of her imagination. Deliberately, she finished off the tequila. It burned all the way to her empty stomach. The nuns, no doubt, were saying novenas over her debauched soul now.

She felt a man stop behind her. "Let's go," he said to her reflection.

"Get lost."

His eyes narrowed. "You either walk out with me now or your parents will be identifying you from a toe tag."

"That would be hard," she said, facing him, "since I don't have any." She paused. "Parents, not toes."

She didn't notice his hard eyes soften a fraction as her gaze slid beyond him to Tiny and Ike. They were glaring laser beams across the room and into her face, and she tried not to let it scare her. She didn't know if it was stupidity or nerve that kept her there, but she wanted to experience danger. Live a little on the edge. And this macho hunk in tight jeans wasn't going to stop her. Not tonight. She'd been a good girl all her life and look what it had gotten her. A nice apartment, even nicer friends and co-workers. And absolute, suffocating, *boredom*. At least *this* got her adrenaline running.

She looked back at Angel. "Who made you my protector?"

"Unfortunate timing." He ought to let her suffer with Tiny and Ike, but he couldn't. It meant her survival that he get her out of here. He took a step closer and she flattened her back against the bar, her elbows propped on the top. She gave him a bored look he didn't believe.

"You want me to come, with you?"

His gaze slid suggestively over her and his chiseled lips quirked. "I haven't touched you yet." She inhaled, her gaze faltering, and he slipped closer, slapping his hands on either side of her and leaning down into her face. "And yes, I want you to leave with me."

"No way." He could be an ax murderer for all she knew. Though some inner voice doubted it. Of course, that inner voice had told her this place would be tame.

He gazed into her blue eyes and felt the entire bar watching them. "Are you that willing to die, lady?"

She scoffed. "You're exaggerating."

"Look at Tiny."

She did. A switchblade lay on the table, Tiny's stubby fingers spinning it, yet his gaze was on her. Pride made her lift her chin, glance back to the bartender and order another drink.

Angel's expression sharpened and before she reached for the fresh glass, he grabbed her hand, ducked and tossed her up across his shoulder.

She shrieked.

The club rumbled with low amusement, as if this occurred every night. Angel clamped a hand familiarly on her upper thigh, grabbed her purse and strode to the door, kicking it open and leaving The Rusty Nail. She fought him every step, wiggling and pounding his back, pushing up and doing everything she could to get free. But Angel just kept walking, a slow saunter. His long stride pounded the breath from her lungs.

"Help! Kidnapping!"

"Shut up." His tone was infinitely calm.

"Rape!"

"I've had sex in a lot of ways, baby, but this is next to impossible."

The gravel of the parking lot crunched beneath his boots and he kept walking.

"You son of a bitch!"

"That's likely."

He stopped and hoisted her off his shoulder, letting his hands smooth provocatively over her thighs and buttocks as he lowered her to her feet.

Calli stumbled on the uneven ground, red-faced with outrage as she drew back her arm. She slapped him, hard. He didn't flinch, didn't blink as her handprint blossomed on his face, and Calli realized he'd allowed her to do it.

"Happy?"

"No."

Without taking his gaze from her, he opened her purse and rummaged for a key. She gasped, trying to take it back, but he held it out of her reach.

"Behave," he warned, her hotel and car keys in his hand. He tossed the purse at her chest and she caught it.

"Give those to me."

He didn't, and moved beside her, hunching down to unlock the car door. His face was inches from hers. "Get in."

Calli blinked, then looked down. "How did you know it was mine?"

He smirked. "Wild guess."

Angel walked around to the driver's side and opened the door. When she didn't move, he propped his arm on the door frame and studied her. She was fire-breathing mad; her small fists clenched, her features tight. He couldn't resist goading her. "Hey, I can drive away in this fifty-thousand dollar car, alone, or you can come with me."

She yanked open the door, glaring at him as she dropped into the seat, venting her anger by slamming the door. He'd ruined everything. She'd just wanted to cross the line into the danger zone and he was bent on playing chaperone. Terrific. At this rate, her tombstone would likely read, "Here lies the vestal virgin, untouched by any man." Or by any excitement.

"I should have you arrested."

"Good luck finding a cop around here." He started the engine and left the lot, swinging by a motorcycle long enough to lock it down and unclip the helmet from the seat. He tossed it into the back of the car and drove away.

Calli huffed and stared out the window. She wasn't afraid of him. Maybe because he had come to her defense, even though she'd had the situation under control. Calli sunk into the seat a little, the truth finding her. Who was she fooling? Outnumbered to start with, Tiny would have pounded her into the concrete like a toothpick into a stick of butter if Angel hadn't stepped in. The fact irked her.

She slanted a quick look at her rescuer. He was so annoyingly calm when she wanted to kick something, preferably him. Well. There was always tomorrow, Sir Galahad. She hadn't come all the way from Texas just to spend her time watching TV. She could go back to the Nail or some other dive anytime.

He drove without talking, but Calli could hear his breathing, smell the scent of him. Not cologne, but a fragrance like nothing she knew. Wind and freedom—and risk. She cast a look at him. He was glancing at her legs. She inched the skirt down.

"Anyone ever tell you that you're a bully?"

"Yeah."

"Arrogant?"

A pause, then, "Yeah."

"A lousy conversationalist?"

He slanted her a quick glance, the hard line of his mouth quirking a fraction.

"Sexy?"

His lips tightened. "I don't want anything from you—" He shot her a confused look. "You got a name?"

"Should have asked that when you decided to play Tarzan and throw me over your shoulder."

"I could have thrown you to the wolves instead."

"I would have survived."

He snorted. "Tiny isn't so tiny when he's pushed, *lady.*"

She caught the demand for her name. She ignored it. He grabbed her purse, yanking it when she tried to take it, digging one-handed until he found her wallet. He flipped it open, sliding a glance at the name, then her.

"Hey, Calli."

Oh, God, that voice was to die for, low and raspy. Annoyed by the thought, Calli grabbed back her things, wishing she could hit him. But he was driving. And she wasn't stupid enough to get herself killed because she was feeling manipulated. Feeling? It was more like being bulldozed by a rampaging demigod of badness.

He slowed the car to a halt and shut off the motor, removing the key and tossing it, with her hotel key, into her lap. He grabbed his helmet from the back seat and met her gaze. "Stay out of the Nail. You don't belong."

Before she could respond with something scathing, he left the car, slamming the door before walking quickly away. She watched him, admiring his taut behind in tight jeans, the long lope of his stride, then she dragged her gaze to her surroundings. She was at her hotel. She looked down at the label on her hotel key.

Calli smacked the dashboard.

God, she hated being patronized by men. Every man at the

factory, even Daniel O'Hara, her boss, liked playing a father figure. If she'd had parents, they would likely have done it, too. Her
seven chefs hovered over her as if she couldn't get dressed without help and if any man became interested in her and wasn't the
epitome of quality, The Boys did their best to destroy him.

People looked at her and saw a "good girl" raised by nuns,
with the morals of a saint, though the latter was a slight exag-
geration. Obviously the dark Angel had seen it, too. Though one
look at him and any morals she'd learned had gone straight out
with the used holy water. Oh, she was grateful that men didn't
think she was easy, and she supposed there were *still* some
women who wouldn't mind the Goody Two-shoes, picket fence,
P.T.A.-domestic goddess image. But Calli loathed it. She hated
how guys cleaned up the conversation when she entered a room,
the jokes dying before the punch line. Or worse, clammed up
altogether. She wanted people to say *exactly* what they were feeling.

Even the men she'd managed to find the time to date recently
were agonizingly polite, obsequious. And painfully dull. They
didn't talk to her, they *chatted,* as if she couldn't handle anything
remotely stressing. If they only knew her past, she thought with
a flash of memory. Calli wanted more. Of what, she wasn't sure.

She felt extraordinarily restrained by the image she *needed* to
project for her career and the one struggling for escape. She
looked down at her clothes and smirked. This wasn't exactly her
usual style, but she felt incredibly daring and lush in leather. And
beneath it all was a wild assortment of Brazilian lingerie that
made her feel gloriously wicked. That was her only private jus-
tice, like snubbing the world when she wore tailored designer
suits. For beneath every one of them was unchained seduction in
lace and garters.

For an instant, she wondered if Angel knew, since he'd had
his hand halfway up her skirt when he'd carted her out of the bar.

She slid over the gearshift and jammed in the key. The engine
revved and she was turning to look behind her when the car door
suddenly opened. Before she could speak, he reached across and
turned off the car, then pulled her too easily from behind the
wheel.

Where had he come from? she wanted to know. She'd watched him walk away!

He held her by the arms to his eye level. "Are you trying to get yourself killed?"

His eyes were like shaved ice. Scary. "Of course not."

"Then what the hell were you doing?" He shook her and one of her shoes plopped to the ground.

"That's not your business, now is it, *Angel*?" Where he got that name, she couldn't begin to wonder. He was more like Lucifer. Dark, lean, with lots of muscle beneath that jean jacket. She felt it when he'd carried her so humiliatingly from the bar. She saw it now in his hauntingly pale eyes. God, they were like crystals, sparkling with secrets. The power of them worried her.

"Do you mind?" She brought her shoeless toe to the crotch of his jeans.

"Don't play there, little tigress," he rasped, and something ignited inside Calli.

"I hadn't planned on it. Well-placed kicks work so much better." She tapped him lightly and his eyes flared. "Put me down."

He did, abruptly, releasing her as if his hands were burned, and stepping back.

Jamming on her loose shoe, she slid back into her car. She didn't look at him, but she could feel him; his stance casual, his hips slanted, thumbs hooked in his belt loops. And those eyes. "I don't know what possessed you to interfere in my life, Angel Whoever-you-are, but I can take care of myself." Where was that car key?

"I'll remember that when I'm reading about your murder in tomorrow's paper."

"You're being a tad possessive toward someone you don't know." She found the key.

Angel watched her search for the ignition, three times. "You're drunk. Miss Thornton."

She held up her hand. "Let's not beat around the bush, shall we? I'm smashed."

"And who will you kill on the road just to spite me?"

She sighed, slowly lowering her head to the steering wheel. The horn beeped and she flinched. He was right, of course. Pride and rebellion could be taken only so far. Removing her keys, she swung her legs to the left and climbed from the BMW, closing the door. The following silence hung like a knife between them, sharp and dangerous.

She stared up at him. His face was expressionless. She didn't think anyone could do that, wipe every ounce of emotion from his face, but he had. She staggered a bit, then bent and took off her shoes. Angel's eyes flared as she straightened.

She was just a little thing.

"Don't let my size mislead," she said, recognizing his surprise. "I really am tougher than I look."

"Same goes here."

She let her gaze rip and slide over him, down to the dark, snakeskin boots, then back up, smiling at the gold loop in his ear. "I can't imagine how." She turned and pointed her oblong key chain at the car. The lights went off, the locks snapped and the alarm set with a double beep. She leveled a side glance at him. "Bet you wish you could lock me up that well, huh, Angel?"

Yes, he thought. He did. But what he wanted was to lock himself up with her.

"G'night, Angel, honey."

She brushed past him as she headed straight to the hotel, her shoes dangling from her fingertips like dainty slippers. His gaze swept her, clinging to her behind shifting inside the leather until she slipped into the hotel room. God, she was one wild number, he thought. No, he corrected, she was playing at being wild. That she hadn't bothered to set the car alarm outside the Nail told him she'd no idea where she was sticking that pretty nose and was damn lucky that her car hadn't been stripped when they'd come out. If she knew anything about The Rusty Nail, she wouldn't have set one polished toe in there. He'd read her instantly when she had. Her clothes were too expensive, too tailored. They spoke of money. And her white BMW screamed it.

He leaned against a street lamp, watching until her lights went out. Then he hitchhiked a ride back to the Nail for his bike. Go home, Calli Thornton, he thought with a ride past the hotel and a final look-see for her car. A good woman like that didn't belong here. Ever. And certainly not near him.

* * *

Gabriel "Angel" Griffin knew he shouldn't get too close to her. Just her perfume drove him mad. God, everything about her drove him nuts. She was sensual energy and didn't realize it. He'd spent the past two nights trying to reason her into a neat isolated corner of his mind. He had to, had to go back to feeling the way he had before he'd laid eyes on her.

*Like nothing.*

*Feeling old and empty at thirty?*

Or keep worrying over a black-haired beauty with a sultry walk and eyes as bright as a New Mexico sky? He wished he could dismiss her from his mind, but he couldn't. He'd made a promise.

And as he relaxed on the seat of his bike, boots propped on the handlebars, he kept one eye peeled on the entrance to Damien's Haven. She was really pushing it this time. Damien's looked like the average yuppie nightclub on the outside; tasteful decor, a bouncer and a line to get in. But inside, it was a designer-draped cesspool. More drug traffic went through that place than a Colombian cartel, bringing out the wired and weird. And Calli was in the center of it.

Last night it was the streets, conversations with people who would sell their souls—and hers—for a few bucks. He'd been there, too, she just hadn't known it. For three days he'd watched her push the limits of her safety; a couple of fairly harmless admirers getting a little too familiar with that sweet behind, a kid trying to snatch her purse, unsuccessfully. So far nothing serious, not that every man within sight came to her rescue just because of her looks and the payback they might receive. The paybacks brought him out of hiding and under her nose tonight.

Rooting in his pockets, he found a half-crushed cigarette and slid it between his lips. Then he hunted for a match, lit it, cupping the flame and squinting through the smoke at the entrance to Damien's. It was wide and he could scrutinize at least two-thirds of the club from here. And her. Or he would be inside right now. He drew on the smoke, exhaling in a short stream, then made a face at the stale taste and pitched it into the street. He saw her move through the club and his chest tightened unfamiliarly as she neared. She paused at the entrance, shaking her head to someone he couldn't see, then left. She maintained even steps and Angel wondered if she'd had anything to drink tonight. She hadn't the past two nights.

She strode toward her car and he enjoyed the sight of those high-heeled legs. It was leather night again. This time, flame red. He liked it. Then she saw him and stopped in the center of the street. Horns beeped and traffic moved around her. The street-lights showered a dingy yellow over her and she continued, pausing briefly to let a car pass.

"How much do you get for baby-sitting?" she called.

He arched a brow, his gaze gliding heavily over her. "You're no baby."

She cocked her hip and smiled. "Nice of you to notice."

"Hard not to."

He liked the faint blush stealing into her face. He couldn't remember the last time he'd seen one. A real one.

"You're becoming a pest. Don't you have a life, a wife, or somewhere else to be?"

Slowly he shook his head. She walked toward him and stopped beside the bike. She planted one hand on her hip and looked him over so thoroughly, Gabe felt his groin tighten. God. Did she know what she did to a man? She was temptation incarnate and Gabe knew he couldn't do what he was thinking. He swung his boots off the handlebars and sat upright.

But just the same, he let his thoughts multiply. And he ended up with her image parading through his mind without a stitch of clothing.

"You're cramping my style, Angel."

He didn't like that she called him that. It wasn't his real name. Some whore on the street gave it to him after his first lay when he was fourteen and he could never shake it. After so many years, he let it ride. But right now, he hated it and wanted to hear her call him Gabe. He shifted, straddling the bike. "Get on."

Her look was bland. "Get real." She moved toward her car, turning off the alarm and opening the locks. He started the motorcycle, riding up beside her and blocking her from opening the door. The noise of the engine settled low.

She sent him an annoyed look. "I don't need rescuing."

"Are you admitting you did the other night?"

"I'll admit to being drunk and nothing more."

"Puked all night, did you?"

She blinked, all innocence and smiles. "My, how attractive of you to mention it."

He smirked, looked away for a second, then stilled, his gaze somewhere beyond her. "Make some interesting friends tonight?" He inclined his head to Damien's and the three men hanging around the doorway. She looked.

"Damn!" Fear—real fear—colored her voice as two of the three men pushed away from the wall and headed toward them. One took a drag on a joint, then snuffed it in his palm and shoved it into his pocket before stepping off the curb. Real bad company, Gabe thought, remembering one of them from the newspaper. But Gabe recognized the look as their eyes traveled over her, her expensive car. She was ready cash for them and nothing more. Then they spotted him.

"Get on, Calli."

"Look, Angel. I don't need your protection." She leaned in, her face inches from his, her hand on her car door handle. "Go find someone who does."

She was just too close, he thought. He wanted to taste her. All of her.

His lips tightened into a grim line as she tried opening the door, giving him an impatient glare to move his bike. Then her gaze darted frantically beyond him to the men.

"Don't be a hero, Calli." He could tell she was scared. "You can't handle them and you know it."

"I wouldn't have to, if you'd move that hunk of steel!" She jerked on the door.

Without another word, Gabe slapped his arm around her waist and dragged her across his lap. Her legs kicked up, her elbow driving into his stomach, her fist immediately clipping him on the chin and knocking his teeth together, stunning him. But he was stronger and faster and wrestled the keys from her fist, then booted the car door shut and rode away. He twisted slightly and set the alarm, then waved at the men in the street.

She grappled for balance and he hoisted her tightly between his thighs.

Calli glared at him.

Gabe rubbed his chin. "Not a bad left cross," he said, amused.

Her lip curled in an unattractive snarl. He dumped her keys into her lap and she scrambled before they fell to the asphalt.

Calli made a frustrated sound. "This is kidnapping, you know."

He glanced to the left as traffic moved alongside him. "Sue me."

"I hate you."

"Good."

Was that supposed to please her? "You are by far the stubbornnest, most irritating man I've ever met."

The wind smoothed her hair back and on the short stretch to the next light, he slumped comfortably in the seat. "Lucky you." He'd met worse, a lot worse. "You didn't cross your pals, yet. *I* could be an angel." He flashed her a grin that looked more like a shark baring its teeth before a kill.

And she'd had enough of him. "Stop. Stop!"

"Calli—?"

"I said stop, dammit!"

He pulled the bike to the side of the street.

Calli shifted, facing him, casually draping her legs over his thigh as if they were in a living room and he was the sofa. "Why do you keep kidnapping me, butting in where you're not wanted?"

Gabe let his gaze slide over her legs, the skirt hiked up so that he could see the tops of her red stockings, lace, and the shadow between. He swallowed and kept his hands away from her. "Because I was watching a lamb walk into a slaughter. Again."

"A lamb? Me?" She tapped her chest, tapered nails clicking against the zipper of her jacket.

He gestured to the street. "You see any other senseless female walking into the sludge of humanity without a thought to her life?"

She reared back, frowning. "I wouldn't call them sludge, exactly, and what do you care about my life? You don't even know me.''

"I know I don't want to be identifying you from—''

She put up a hand. "I get the picture—a toe tag.''

Calli avoided his gaze, wondering how she was going to dump him and still avoid those other "friends.''

But Gabe saw the cogs moving behind those expressive eyes and said, "Night's over, Cal.''

Her gaze slid to his, deep blue challenging white-green. Calli knew she would lose. He would camp out on her doorstep and play he-man if she didn't go to bed meekly. She didn't know how she knew that, but she did.

She threw her legs off his and straddled the bike, trying unsuccessfully to keep her skirt down.

He heard the bitterness in her voice when she said, "Then take me home, bad boy.''

Gabe leaned forward, her back pressed to his chest and he ached to run his hands up those legs and beneath the leather skirt. "You wouldn't know bad,'' he whispered in her ear, "if it was right behind you.''

She turned her head, meeting his piercing gaze head-on. "Is that so?''

"Yeah. Or you wouldn't be riding with me.''

"Like I have a choice?''

He gunned the engine, spitting pebbles as he shot away from the curb. Her body mashed back against his and he slipped one arm around her waist. Her breath caught, then released slowly, and Gabe liked the soft, shuddering sound he felt rather than heard.

But he didn't like how satisfying she felt in his arms. Or how much he craved it when he'd gone without human contact for so long. The temptation for more told him to send her packing, now. And the only reason this trusting female would split, was if she realized she'd trusted the wrong kind of man. He wasn't supposed to like her, just keep her sweet butt from ending up on a slab. That's all he was being paid for, nothing else.

# TWO

They rode in silence, the wind whipping at their clothes, dust curling behind the Harley. His arm tightened around her waist as he tipped the bike on a turn. The big machine vibrating between her legs had nothing to do with her quickening breath. It was him, all him. Tucked snugly behind her, his thighs encasing hers, she felt like she was wearing him. His hand lay splayed across her stomach and she sensed every digit, his wide palm, his arm curling around her hip. Calli hadn't experienced anything quite this powerful in her life and she closed her eyes, wishing she could control her reaction to him. But this was what she'd wanted. Risk. Danger.

The wind friction did nothing to hide the sound of his breathing in her ear. She didn't try talking to him. But then his hand shifted as their speed increased, moving a fraction lower and with her legs spread, she experienced a sudden rush of heat. He must have sensed it, disliked it, for he immediately brought his hand to the steering grip. Then a moment later, he guided the bike into a parking lot. Her hotel again, she thought grimly as he pulled the

Harley in front of her room. Above them neon lights flashed Vacancy.

He shoved the kickstand down and shut off the motor. The blunted silence strained the taut wire between them and she didn't turn to look at him, watching his hand flex on the grip before it lowered to remove the key.

She felt him pocket the key and she shifted on the narrow seat, meeting his gaze. Something moved beneath those ice-green eyes before the look was shuttered to emptiness. He appeared relaxed, arms folded over his chest, his back braced on the bar, his legs spread. Her gaze followed the line from thigh to his flat stomach, then up to his face. His lips quirked. She stared him down, her chin lifting a bit. She could admire a good-looking man if she wanted, she thought petulantly. She might have been raised in a Catholic orphanage, but she was, by no means, a nun.

She shifted between his legs, her buttocks brushing the insides of his thighs as she slid her leg over the bike. She stood and the ground rolled. How could one drink, hours ago, make her feel this dizzy?

"You look a little pale."

Was that concern in his voice real? "Actually, I had only one drink around seven, but I feel like I'm going to wretch."

His brows furrowed for a split second. "Not on me." He gave her a soft shove toward her room.

She took a couple of steps, then cocked a look at him. He was admiring her behind and she'd caught him at it. So. He wasn't as indifferent as he seemed.

"Want to come in?" *Careful, Calli.*

"And watch you get sick?"

Her smile mocked. "What'sa matter, Angel, honey. Afraid?"

"You should be."

"Of you?" Her brows lifted. "You've got to be kidding. You're as tame as they come under all that—" She waved loosely at the motorcycle and knew it was a lie.

His expression didn't change and she faced him fully, sauntering closer, so close she smelled the untouchable wildness surrounding him. He didn't budge a muscle, only his gaze followed her. She laid her hand on his thigh and muscle tensed beneath. But still, he didn't move.

"Back off, Calli," came the low rasp. "You don't know what you're getting into."

Her gaze challenged him. "What will you do, Angel? Chew me up and spit me out?" Her face neared his, the whisper of her breath on his lips. Her gaze never wavered, searching his and waiting for a reaction. But he was as lifeless as a granite statue. The temptation of his stillness, to make him respond, urged her on. She let her mouth hover over his, let him feel her nearness like an animal scents its prey.

"What will you do, bad boy?" Her words moistened his lips.

His gaze thinned, pale with a predatory gleam, and her bravado fled.

She abruptly pulled back and walked briskly to her room. She inserted the key, turned the knob and opened the door.

Suddenly he was there, behind her, one arm around her waist, the other hand slapping open the door. "See, little tigress?" he rasped in her ear. "You don't know what danger is." He twisted her around. "It *was* right behind you."

"Angel?" Panic swam in her voice as she stared into his fathomless eyes.

A wound flickered across his features, then left.

Suddenly he ducked, his mouth a hard slash across hers, his kiss heavy and demanding. Disillusionment ripped through her. She deserved this for teasing him, trusting him, and even as savage heat scored through her, she pushed at his shoulders, his chest, tried tearing her mouth away. But he followed, exacting a response. She tried not to give it, fighting the greedy feel of his mouth, his hands running over her body. Still he kissed her and kissed her, his advancing body urging her farther into the room, back against a short dresser. Bodies meshed, hard planes pushing to soft skin.

His kiss was unrelenting and laced with dangerous consequences. Tempting.

Calli's body was already betraying her, her skin dampening, and even as she gripped his jacket to push him back, she fought a war inside herself between outrage and hurt—and the glorious pressure of his warm wet mouth on hers. It coupled with a strange hunger in his kiss, a tight restraint daring her to join him and, without warning, her lips softened beneath his, immediately eager.

Angel jerked back, his potent glare clashing with hers. She met and matched it, all mutinous. *You started this,* her gaze challenged. Their breathing was labored, bodies aroused to unthinkable heights. And he pushed the limit.

He grasped her hips and ground her to his hardness, his mouth to hers.

Like Ike had tried. But this wasn't the same. Nothing was. Galvanizing sensations pelted her again and again, nothing repulsive, all primitive and devouring. Calli knew she'd never experienced anything this forceful; domination of her body and mind. She thought she would go mad if she didn't have more.

Then he gave it, insinuating his knee between hers and maneuvering her onto the dresser. One hand dove into her hair, holding her for the burn of his kiss while his free hand slid heavily over her chest, pulling at her jacket zipper and spreading the leather. Beneath it, he found a shapely bustier and his fingertips made contact with bare skin as they closed over her breast. He squeezed, driving his thumb beneath the satiny fabric and wildly flicking her tender nipple.

A trapped sound scraped her throat.

He tore his mouth from hers and she heard his breath rush past her ear before he ground his lips to her neck, nipping, licking, urging her head back. She clutched fistfuls of his jacket. Breath panted. He deliberately licked a path from her throat to the swells of her breasts. His big hands spanned her rib cage, covered it, then sank lower, molding over her hips to the edge of her skirt. He paused for a fraction, red stockings and flesh beneath his palms, and she tipped her head. Calli quaked, her entire body brimming with pure energy about to detonate. Her gaze drifted upward to meet pale, hooded eyes.

Her fingers flexed on his shoulders.

Her breath mingled damply with his.

And he swallowed it, his mouth devouring hers, more sensual than consuming. More hunger than heat. She didn't know which was more powerful. That, or his hands roaming upward beneath her skirt, fingertips curling behind and enveloping her buttocks.

A dark groan sounded in his throat.

She wore a thong and Gabe touched naked skin.

It nearly destroyed him.

He could have her now, he thought. Any way he wanted. She was open, vulnerable—and innocent. He could take her body coldly in a couple of thrusts and leave her. Show her no one was trustworthy enough for someone like her. Especially him. That a woman like Calli, a good woman, felt *anything* for a man like him was beyond his comprehension. That he wanted desperately to touch her with the deliberation of a welcomed lover was the real danger. Yet even as the image of being inside her made him shudder with a nearly uncontrollable need, he knew he had to destroy this.

"You want it, baby?" His words thrummed against her lips before he kissed them with designed torture. And she responded. Yeah, like leading a lamb to slaughter, he thought. His fingers flexed on her buttocks, drawing a flood of moisture from her. She shifted, restless. "Do you?"

Calli whimpered, her thoughts clouded, her body combustible.

His arm snaked around her waist, fusing them as tightly as if they were naked and joined. His mouth against her ear, he whispered, "I could have you now, baby, and you'd never see me again."

She blinked at the sudden cruelty in his voice. Then he spoke again, harsh and vulgar, telling her what he wanted, using crude words she'd read or heard, but never directed at herself.

"No!" She shoved at his chest, turning her face away, but he kept on. Calli twisted and pushed, her sensual dream shattering with every syllable like arrows fired into her composure. He wouldn't let her go and she turned her head sharply, sinking her teeth into his tender neck. He hissed and lurched back, covering the spot, checking for blood. Their eyes met, hers filled with humiliation and disappointment, his cold and flat.

In blatant contempt, she wiped the back of her hand across her mouth.

He reached over and caught her jaw in his broad hand, fingers biting into her flesh. "Go home, little girl, this is not your play-ground." He kissed her, hard, lacking even a hint of apology. "It's mine." He turned away, and without looking back, strode to the door. He didn't stop, even when the vase shattered against the doorjamb by his head.

Calli glared at the empty doorway, shoving hair from her face. Then she looked down at herself and choked back a sob, pushing unsteadily off the dresser. She closed her jacket, her body still thrumming with desire as she staggered to the door. Her shattered equilibrium threatened her every step. She kicked the broken vase outside and slammed the door shut. Closing her eyes, she leveled a few nasty curses at Angel and hoped she'd severed his jugular. *God, I am such a fool,* she thought. She deserved whatever she got.

She passed the mirror, her gaze catching her reflection. Her bruised lips curled in disgust. Her eyes were bleary, her hair a tangled mess. Her clothes suffocated her and she stripped them off, dropping them to the floor as she moved toward her bed. She sat heavily, springs creaking.

Deep inside her, an old wound broke open, fresh hurt rubbing raw. For an instant she was a child left in darkness with strangers. Damn. She squeezed her eyes shut, tears eeking past. He'd hu-miliated her with her own reaction to him, intentionally, she knew. But somewhere during his attempt to scare her, she'd ex-perienced something wild and raw. And so had he. Part of her admitted that, for several moments there, she'd wanted him, would have done anything to feel his strength and do exactly what he'd whispered in her ear. Another part wanted to beat him sense-less, hurt him back.

*Don't trust him. He's bad,* a voice said. The nuns had warned her about men like Angel. Dangerous men. Men women went after just because they were tough and hard and without regret. He didn't want anyone to hurt her, except him. She looked up, her eyes narrowing on nothing.

He didn't want her to trust anyone, *including* him.

Just as the thought materialized, so did a wave of nausea and Calli slapped a hand over her mouth, leaping toward the bathroom. Tomorrow, she thought. She would deal with her stupidity tomorrow. She only hoped she would *never* see him again.

Sunlight blared through a slice between the drapes and Calli groaned, rolling to her side and covering her head with a pillow. Her mouth tasted like road dust and her brain throbbed, reminding her of last night. How could one drink make her feel this crummy?

After a few deep breaths, she slithered from the bed like the idiot she was, stopping long enough to order coffee from room service before stepping into the shower. She didn't bother to regulate the water and suffered the ice-cold blast before making it warmer. She never wanted to leave. It was safe under the water, away from the hurt blooming slowly in her chest. *Damn you, Angel.*

Gradually, her headache lessened and she could actually move without making it worse. *No,* she decided as pain buffeted her brain. She would stay in here, because looking at herself in the mirror would only relive the memory of Angel's heartlessness. Funny, she thought, that she could remember his passion more than his cruelty.

Gabe caught the waiter as he made to set the tray by the door. She's in the shower, he realized instantly, hearing the running water through the paper-thin walls and half-open window. Pushing a hefty tip into the server's palm, he took the tray and gave the teenager a leer that spoke volumes. The youth smiled and nodded, then after a moment's hesitation, unlocked the room.

Gabe set the tray down and closed the door. He noticed her clothes scattered over the floor and collected them in a pile, trying to ignore the red stocking shaped from her leg and the memories that came with it. Tossing them onto the dresser, he wondered why the hell he was here. Sure, he could have left her car at Damien's, let her find a way to get it back, but Gabe felt as if he'd slunk out from under a rock, like the slimy perverts he'd been protecting her from for the past four days.

Since last night, he'd focused his concern on the one drink she claimed to have had and the strange result. After discreetly taking her keys, in case she got any wild ideas during the night, he'd gone back to Damien's after leaving her, done some checking, and linked her artificial intoxication to a drink she hadn't bought for herself. A man of vague description had walked it over to her from the bar. It was just too suspicious for Gabe's comfort and he felt that her *admirer* might have slipped her a drug.

Calli was in trouble, more than she'd ever hoped to find. And if she would quit trusting strangers, quit trying to find danger, it just might not find her. Gabe muttered a curse, hating himself for what he'd done to her, hating that he couldn't find another way around her stubbornness to keep her safe. She was just too willing to test the limits of the wrong people. Including him.

The phone rang and instinctively he snatched it up.

"Yeah?"

"What are you doing there at this hour?" Daniel O'Hara demanded.

"My job." Gabe stared down at her keys in his hand, then clutched them in his fist. "Did you find anything else?"

"No. Does she know who you are?"

Guilt stabbed through Gabe as he glanced at the bathroom door. He dismissed it, remembering the disgusted look in her eyes when he'd talked nasty to her. "You paid for discretion."

"Your voice says otherwise, Gabe."

Gabe hated the fatherly warning in Daniel's tone. "Let's just say she won't be trusting me or anyone else for a while."

"It's a sweet failing of hers." A sigh came through the phone and Daniel's worry with it. Whether it was for himself and his company or Calli, Gabe couldn't be sure. "She has the memo."

Gabe groaned, plowing his fingers through his dark hair. "Great." How was he supposed to get it? His gaze scanned the room, stopping on her purse, then a leather satchel lying on a luggage rack. "I'll see what I can find."

"That cat burglar experience comes in handy in your line of work, huh?"

"Shut up, Danny."

Daniel cleared his throat.

"I'll call if I have something to say."

Daniel scoffed. "I'll be old by then."

Gabe made to hang up when Daniel's voice caught him.

"Hey, Gabe?"

He put the phone to his ear again, noticing that the shower had stopped. "Make it quick."

"Don't hurt her. She's like a daughter to me."

Gabe closed his eyes. Wonderful. Daniel might be just the owner of some dessert company, but he was one mean man when crossed. And Gabe owed him big already.

"What are you doing here, talking on *my* phone?" Calli demanded, tightening the sash of her robe.

His expression blank, Gabe held out the receiver. "Someone named Daniel?"

Calli's features reddened and she grabbed the phone, turning her back on him. She could feel Angel's gaze move over her terry-cloth robe and she pushed it higher around her neck. While in the bathroom, she'd heard muffled voices and could have sworn Angel was talking to Daniel long before she entered the room. But what would he have to say to her boss? Daniel was likely giving him the third degree, she decided, highly annoyed with both of them.

"How did you find me?" she snapped, her plan to hide out in New Mexico obviously ruined.

His laugh was soft. "Well, hello to you, too." Calli made an apologetic sound. "It wasn't hard. What happened to Acapulco?"

"Nothing. It's still there, I think." She heard him chuckle. "I just changed my mind and decided to drive." She already knew how he'd found her. For emergency's sake she'd left this number with her landlord and Daniel was the one who'd told her about the quaint small town. "Is there something wrong? Why did you track me down?"

There was a hesitation and then, "I was worried when you didn't show at the company suite in Mexico. Your team asked about you."

Daniel was lying and she couldn't for the life of her understand why. "What's the matter?" she asked with soft concern, plowing her wet hair back off her face.

"Nothing, kid. Nothing. Who's the guy?"

Calli glanced back over her shoulder, her eyes narrowing dangerously. Angel was sprawled on her bed, folded arms pillowing his head, ankles crossed. The arrogant creep, she thought. She picked up an ashtray and threw it at him. He batted it away, then resumed his position. She gestured for him to get out.

He simply stared back.

"He's the waiter." His gaze went flat. "A real pest," she said meaningfully. "And I have to get rid of him."

"Be careful, Calli."

Another man playing knight-errant, she thought, and her first impulse was to vent her anger and hurt on Daniel, but he didn't deserve it. He was the best thing to happen to her career since her graduation from the Culinary Institute and she didn't want to dump on him.

"I will," she said finally. "And tell the seven wizards that just because I'm on vacation doesn't mean they are, too."

"I will," Daniel laughed. "'Bye, Calli."

"Later, boss." She hung up, her fingers flexing on the receiver before she shoved them into her robe pockets. She faced Angel. "Get out."

He said nothing, his cool gaze assessing her as if he'd palmed every inch of her naked body.

"You have to know you're the absolute last person I want to see. Or are you just a sadist?" He kept quiet and she wanted to kick him. "Why are you here?"

Leaning up on his elbow, he dangled her keys.

Her forehead wrinkled. She'd had them last night. She was sure of it. "You stole them?"

Angel swung his long legs off the bed and straightened. Calli stepped back, and he arched a brow at the sudden move, studying her.

She was afraid. Good. Lesson achieved.

"You could have left them at the front desk."

Gabe shrugged. Sure, he could have, but he'd needed to see her, needed to see for himself that he hadn't smashed that untouchable energy of hers.

Calli held out her hand and he dropped the keys into her palm. They were warm from handling. She turned away, staring at the keys, then him. He had to have taken them from her purse. She hated to think he'd taken anything else.

As casually as she could, she poured herself a cup of coffee, realizing he'd gotten inside by way of the waiter. She would have to speak to the hotel management about that.

"So, are you a thief, as well as a...molester?"

He stiffened. "The car's outside," he said. The sound of his raspy voice shivered through Calli.

She gulped hot coffee and met his gaze in the mirror. "Leave, Angel."

He moved up behind her. She clutched the cup defensively. "How's your head?"

"What do you care?"

"I don't." He did. But he didn't want to. She was a case, an assignment, nothing more; protect her, get the memo back before Daniel's competitors came after her for it. And if Daniel could find her this easily so could they. Gabe had never guessed the dessert business was so bloodthirsty. "I don't." He shrugged big shoulders. "Just making conversation."

"Should have tried that last night." Instantly Calli wished the words back and set the cup down with a sharp click.

He moved up behind her and still she wouldn't face him. "Wouldn't have been as much fun." God, he nearly puked on those words.

"Jeez," she mumbled, eyes downcast. "I hate to see what you think is pain, then."

Guilt tightened his features and he was glad she wasn't looking at him. Gabe didn't know what possessed him then, but he leaned down and scented her, his face close to the bare nape of her neck. She didn't smell like soap or shampoo, but of Calli, of innocence and energy and life. He wanted some. Just a little to warm his dark dreams. "You liked it."

"You have no idea what I like, Angel, honey. But it certainly isn't you!" Her voice fractured, fresh wounds mirrored in her eyes. "Get out," she sneered.

Angel caught her arms in a gentle hold and pulled her back against him. Calli went still as glass, instantly sensing a difference. His long body was hard against her back, her soft buttocks, and raw desire burst like a newborn star. Calli struggled against it, against the urge to open her robe and let him touch her.

Gabe felt it, too; her quickening breath, the sudden tightness of her small, naked body beneath the thick terry cloth. Blood rushed to his groin. His fingers flexed on her arms. He didn't want to know what she was feeling that easily, didn't want to be such an intense part of it. Yet he turned her to face him, tipping her chin till she looked him in the eye.

His fingers sank into her hair as he covered her mouth with his. Calli immediately fought. But his kiss was different than the last; gentle, probing. Unhurried and seething with suppressed desire. Her heart thundered against the wall of her chest. Her knees softened. Her resistance melted a fraction more, but instinct born in survival, in a little girl left to fend alone years ago, kept her from giving him what he coaxed to the surface.

She tore her mouth away, breathless.

"No. No!" She pushed him back. He went only because he chose to, she knew. Sweet mercy. How could she fall for this again? She leveled a scathing glance at him. "Last night must be fuzzier than I thought, if I keep walking into your traps," she muttered more to herself as she scooted a safe distance from him.

Calli faced the fact that she was highly attracted to him, that she trusted him no matter how hard she tried not to or how serious he was about wanting her gone. Yet even in her confusion, which was threatening to dissolve any guard on her self-preservation, a familiar awareness drew her back to him, to the darkness and secrets he wanted to shield from her, from the world. She promised herself she would fight it. But then she glanced at him and was swallowed in those hard green eyes devouring her willpower like a panther with a defeated victim. His gaze slipped to the neck of the robe, to her skin, and she was acutely aware of her nakedness thinly shielded, aware of him and how erotic his touch felt on her body. Her breathing increased, a deep, pulsing ache spreading up her thighs as he simply looked at her. She broke her gaze, frantically grasping for some anger, some disgust. But it just wasn't there.

Frustrated, she threw her hands up. "All right, I give up. I know when I've been licked."

"So," came the dark rasp. "Last night *is* coming back to you."

She sputtered, swinging around to see him pause at the door, his tanned hand on the frame as he looked at her. An odd half-smile tugged at his lips, his gaze caressing her. White-hot heat spiraled through her, making her mad.

"You're twisted, Angel."

"Remember that."

Calli didn't know what to make of the shadow shifting over his expression.

But Gabe knew. And he was even more certain of himself now. Now that her faint smile offered forgiveness for the despicable cruelty he'd played on her last night. He didn't deserve forgiving, but he was glad he had it. God. He *had* to keep away from her. Touching her brought him a bizarre freedom that he would keep destroying in slow increments until he destroyed her, too.

He wasn't good enough for a woman like Calli. Not for her kisses, her smiles and for damn sure, not her bed.

Southern New Mexico was beautiful, full of exquisite little shops brimming with unique and very expensive items. Calli decided to hurt her credit card. Mega-shopping was an instant balm to her bruised feelings. Angel had vanished and although she decided it was just as well, giving herself time to get her act together, she actually missed his pesty brooding self. She'd had plenty of time to think about him and his invasion into her life. And why he'd bothered to bring her car back, clearly a gallant gesture, when he'd warned her not to trust him? She remembered the crude way he'd spoken to her, his matter-of-fact manner about the scene he played on her. And that's exactly what it was, she thought. A scene. Designed and executed especially for her oh-so-delicate constitution. A warning. He didn't know her well enough to realize that it would take more than his less-than-subtle charm to send her packing.

Sighing dispiritedly, Calli fingered a silk blouse and knew she trusted too easily. The nuns had taught her to see the best in everyone. If she hadn't, she wouldn't have insisted Daniel let her hire Rodrigez straight out of prison. Rodrigez had proven that his prison training was valuable and had become her number one chef. More importantly, though, it had shown she'd been right; there was good in the former armed robber. It was a break she could afford to give now and she understood how infrequently those came along. Like Rodriguez, she had no family and since she was a child, had depended only on herself. Even under the care of very loving but strict nuns, she was always alone. Being a ward of the church until she was eighteen had its moments, albeit very few, but she'd never met anyone as enigmatic and ominous as Angel.

She was attracted to him, by more than the quiet restrained power he exuded. And he scared her, his empty eyes, his vacant expressions. Sometimes, it was like no one lived behind those beautiful pale green eyes. Yet despite her fear, her lack of knowledge about men like him, she was drawn to him, as if only she could feel an invisible lure.

Was it his secrets she found so intriguing? And what had Daniel said to him on the phone? They'd spoken before she entered the room, she was certain. Angel was hiding something. What it had to do with her was beyond comprehension. Or maybe it was as she'd first imagined, Daniel feeling protective and questioning him?

She pushed open the door of a kitchen store and smiled. She was in heaven and moved from rack to shelf, seeking the odd gadget she might not already have in her own kitchen. She hadn't worked in over a week, which meant she hadn't cooked. And she wanted to test out a new recipe batting around in her head. Finding nothing to sufficiently satisfy her buying spree, Calli settled for a red cobbler's apron with the words I Cook, You Clean emblazoned in white. She laughed to herself. Who was going to clean up after her? She lived alone.

Juggling the handles of four bags, Calli left the shop and immediately bumped into a man. She dropped one of her packages and bent to retrieve it just as he did. She thanked him, then straightened and stared into a pair of warm brown eyes.

"Gee, I'm glad I don't have to pay for that loot," he said, gesturing to her bags.

Calli smiled. "I'll hate myself when the bill comes, I just know it." She started past him. "Thank you."

"You look like an expert shopper." He paused and she waited for him to continue. "Think you could help me select something for my sister's birthday?"

Indecision creased her brow. "I don't know…"

"I'm afraid I'm a failure at getting her anything she doesn't return." His tone pleaded.

Calli bit her lower lip. Harmless, she thought, we'll be in public.

"Clothes or jewelry?"

Relieved, he chuckled to himself. "Find me a woman who can resist jewelry and I'll marry her."

She looked him over, smiling. "Sorry, pal, you'll have a long hunt," she said, then gestured to her car. "Let me get rid of these." Leaving her packages in the car, she liked that he kept his distance, remaining on the pathwalk to wait for her. She didn't want this guy too close. Though he seemed nice enough, and in the past week she'd certainly hung out with people who were far more menacing, Angel's warnings vibrated in her mind. Along with the memory of his touch. A soft smile bowed her lips as she walked back to him.

"Something funny? You look, I don't know—" he shrugged "—satisfied?"

Not quite, she thought mischievously, but said, "It's nothing." She gestured up the walk. "I saw a wonderful Indian jewelry display up here." He met her pace and made introductions on the way to the store. Braiden Murdock, engineer, businessman in town for the week, she discovered, and Calli mentally classed him in the "yuppie, financially stable, now-looking-for-a-wife-before-he-got-too-old" department. Especially when he started the conversation with the "Are you married? Don't you want a family?" lines. Like she was on a schedule?

Minding her manners, in minutes Calli had the store owner displaying his creations for Braiden. Calli bought a pair of turquoise cufflinks for Daniel and earrings for herself. As the shopkeeper wrapped items and had them shipped for Braiden, he asked if he could repay her with lunch. Calli stared into his chocolate-brown eyes, thinking he was a gentle, considerate man and she would enjoy his company, but a voice whispering, *He isn't Angel,* interrupted her thoughts. Extremely annoyed with the invasion, she agreed.

A half hour later, she smiled at his wide-eyed look.

"You're a chef?"

"Don't look so surprised. Women can cook, or have you been sleeping for the past two thousand years?"

He laughed quietly, leaning back in his chair and toying with his fork. "So. Give. Where can I try these culinary talents?"

"London, Paris, Rome, New York, Dallas." His brows wrinkled in confusion. "Excalibur Confections," she supplied.

His eyes widened. "The pastries? The ones with the gold sword charm through their centers?"

She nodded. Excalibur was the elite dessert, like Godiva was to chocolates, each dessert wrapped in gold-embossed paper. The gold sword charm was her idea. Customers needed a little pleasure, even after the last bit was gone.

"I eat them whenever I can afford it."

She peered over the edge of the table at his stomach. "Not worried about fat or cholesterol, huh?"

"I run to do penance for those goodies," he said, gesturing for the waiter.

Penance. A Catholic boy, she thought. He paid the check and they left the restaurant. Discreetly, she stepped away from his touch at the small of her back and for an instant wondered why she'd let a guy like Ike paw her as if she were covered in fur, yet wouldn't let Braiden lay a finger on her.

Outside, he waved and a gray limousine slowed to a halt in front of them. Whoa, she thought, more than financially stable.

"Can I give you a lift to your car?"

"The whole thirty yards?" She laughed lightly and shook her head, then offered her hand. He clasped it, tugging her closer. He stood within the open door of the limo.

"Join me for dinner." That it sounded like a demand set her teeth on edge.

"No, thank you, Braiden." She tried to pull free, but his grip tightened. Suspicion crept up her spine.

"Come on." He ducked into the car, making her lean down a bit. Calli caught a glimpse of the plush interior, the bar, TV, laptop computer, and mostly, the mini-fax with a picture of a familiar face curled over the machine. "You already know I don't bite."

"But *she* does."

Calli jerked her hand free and whirled around. Angel. He was braced against the stone wall near the restaurant entrance, one leg bent, booted foot flattened against the wall. His arms folded over his chest, he had *Dare me* written in every taut muscle. Something in her heart said, *Yes!* But her mind scolded her, reason screaming that she shouldn't be so pleased to see his stubbled mug.

His green gaze shifted from her face to her lunch date hanging half out of the limo. Pale eyes glittered and his long legs took him to the side of the car. He loomed over her, sparing her a flash of a look, then maneuvered his body along the limo, making her either step or be pushed back.

"Dammit, Angel!"

His hands braced on the door frame and the roof, he ignored her and peered down at the man, studying him briefly. From what Calli could see, Braiden simply stared back.

"She's busy."

Calli politely tapped his shoulder.

"Calli, are you all right with this?" Braiden asked.

Gabe smirked.

Calli wanted to punch Braiden herself, but Angel blocked her. "It's all right," she said tiredly. She ought to be used to Angel butting in by now.

Gabe leaned down into Braiden's face, his voice so low she couldn't hear.

"Try that again," he rasped, each word clipped and razor sharp as his gaze, "and I *will* kill you."

The other man's features stretched tight. Message received, Angel thought, then stepped back and made to close the door, forcing Braiden to jerk his legs inside or be crushed. The limo peeled away from the curb. Gabe watched it leave the posh galleria, then turned to Calli. She was already walking to her car.

His gaze swept the body-shaping, lemon-yellow tank dress to her tanned bare legs and yellow-heeled shoes. His breath hissed out between clenched teeth. She looked good enough to eat.

His gaze shot to the limo. That was too damn close. It was only pure luck that he'd hung around a little longer than he'd planned. She hadn't a clue, he decided, and wondered what she would think if she knew her *friend* had been trying to kidnap her.

# Three

She really had a sweet behind, he thought before he stirred himself and started toward her.

"Be warned, Angel," she said the instant he was near. "I won't be responsible for what I may say—" Her gaze slid meaningfully to the teeth marks she'd left on his neck. "Or do right now." She unlocked her car and slid into the seat.

But he stopped her from closing the door. He noticed that her hands shook.

She glared up at him. "Do you mind?" He gave her that passionless stare she was beginning to really hate, his long body bent, hand on the car roof. She sighed back into the seat and spoke to the ceiling. "You have made this my worst vacation in years."

"Slumming wasn't good enough, so you went after bigger game?" He nodded toward the restaurant.

She was insulted and her look told him she was fresh out of patience. "I realize this may come as a complete shock, Angel. But I'm not on a manhunt. In fact, after this week, the last thing I want is another man in my life. I have at least eight—no." She put up a hand. "Make that nine," she added, delivering a glare that carved the flesh from his bones. "Nine men who can't keep to themselves and leave me alone!"

She jerked on the door handle, but still he wouldn't move.

"Do I have to hurt you?"

He straightened. "Listen, little tigress," he said. "Your lunch date was—"

"Trying to get me into his limo by force?"

His brows rose.

Her smug look slapped him. "I'm not a fool. Money tends to breed arrogance." Her gaze swept him. "But that doesn't seem to stop you, now, does it?"

She was still smarting, he thought. Calli wasn't a mean person. He'd known that from the start. Though she didn't know why Braiden Murdock was trying to steal her away, Gabe recognized the fact that Calli wasn't leaving, no matter how much he wanted her to go home, where it would be safe. She was his job, his responsibility, and he had only one choice left. Close off any danger.

"Come home with me."

Her eyes narrowed sharply. "Excuse me?" She tipped her head toward him, cupping her ear. "Did I hear right?" She lowered her hand. "You, who wanted me gone from your precious little town, are inviting me into the wolf den, the *love* dungeon?"

He liked the way she teased him. As if she expected to get a rise with her soft-soaped barbs. "No, I'm not. I'm inviting you to *work* for me."

Work for him? As what? His personal sex slave? "I have a job."

"You haven't heard the offer."

There was heat in that statement, she thought, tempting heat.

"And you don't know my qualifications."

He squatted inside the open door, the air suddenly filled with her perfume. He inhaled the soft, powdery fragrance, gazing into her eyes. He braced his forearms on his thighs and clenched his fists in an effort not to touch her. He didn't know why he was doing this. There had to be other choices if he thought long enough. Getting close to a woman like her was dangerous for him. She was the past he never had. The tender heart and passion he'd never known, never even been close to. But the side of him that survived by sheer luck and deviousness on the streets said to risk it, invite her into his world and see if he could hang with it.

"I'm shorthanded for the next couple of weeks and—"

"What is it that you do?" she interrupted.

He couldn't tell her he paid more bills as a private investigator than with the profits from his ranch. Not that she would be any help at either. He didn't want her getting suspicious. He'd already screwed up by talking to Daniel where she could overhear.

"I have a small farm in the valley."

She blinked, her wide eyes looking him over. "You? A farmer? Oh, please." She rolled those big blue eyes and Gabe fought a smile. Smart-ass to the end.

He shrugged and muscles twisted beneath his tight black T-shirt. "It's just as well, a woman like you—" he indicated the expensive car and clothes with a quick flick of his hand "—probably couldn't cut it on a farm."

Rebellion lit her features, her incredible lake-blue eyes. He'd expected it, counted on it, and as she leaned close he had the irresistible urge to kiss the tightness out of her lush little mouth.

"You have no idea what I can *cut*."

Gabe smirked. "There's no electricity, no phones, just work." He said it like a taunt. He could see the indecision in her face. Something wild scrambled in his chest as he waited for her to answer. He shouldn't want this, this bad. It was like inviting a sweet little lamb into the lion's den again and asking it not to run for cover. And asking the lion not to trespass. He straightened, staring down at her. God, she was beautiful.

Calli had never been on a farm. Not that she wasn't used to hard, backbreaking work. The nuns had seen to that when she was old enough to scrub a floor. But spending time with him would be more than hard work. It would be agony. She turned her attention to the emblem on her steering wheel. If she looked at him she couldn't think clearly. Why she was even considering his offer was totally irrational. But she also considered that guys like Ike and Tiny were afraid of him. She should be, too, she thought, after the other night. Yet she wasn't. He'd had the opportunity to hurt her and hadn't.

Though she'd asked around town about him, no one knew who she was talking about and she let it drop. But what pressed her to even contemplate his offer was what she'd seen in Murdock's limo. The face on the fax sheet was hers. That meant he'd singled her out. Why? She could only assume it was because of Excalibur and the competitors' constant offers for her to leave Daniel and come work for them. She'd refused and she'd believed that force was beyond them. Apparently that wasn't the case. It made her distrust everyone. Except Angel. At least she knew where he was coming from. Well, almost. She didn't think anyone knew him at all. And never would.

And farming? She knew what to do with the stuff once it came to market, but cultivating it? Other than growing herbs on her balcony, she was out of her league. But then, if she was away, really out of touch, maybe Daniel and his seven cohorts would get a dose of reality. She could take care of herself. And they needed to know it or she couldn't go back to Excalibur to work. Their smothering was half the reason she'd taken her first vacation in three years and hadn't told them where she was really going. And a woman could take only so much shopping and bars and self-imposed solitude. Besides, she did have her car and portable phone if she needed to connect.

She tilted a look at him and still couldn't decide. It was an almost too-dangerous offer. "Let me think about it."

He released the breath he'd been holding. "Suit yourself." At least she hadn't said no. He would stick around, close, just the same.

"How can I get in touch with you?"

"I'll find you." He moved away from the car.

"Mysterious men are pains in the butt," she muttered to herself, then heard him chuckle. She pulled the car door closed and started the engine. She warned herself not to watch him walk, that long, determined stride, his adorable behind. Except the urge took her. Oh, God, why didn't she just say no and forget the whole idea? Spend time with him, perhaps all alone in a valley, under his beneficiary?

Was she crazy?

Then it struck her that he'd invited her for reasons of his own, that he wanted her with him enough to tolerate her and ignore the desire racing between them. Did he know that with just a glance of those steely green eyes he transformed her into quivering mush? Though it was obvious that she had little effect on him, she thought depressingly. But she knew she had *some* effect. If he thought she believed he was just playing a game, he was the fool, not her. She'd felt the capped fire in him when he'd kissed her the other night, felt the hardness straining his jeans.

Two days ago, Angel wanted her gone so bad he'd tried to scare her out of town.

This morning, Angel wanted her body with the prowess of a determined lover.

This afternoon, he'd been there to squelch anything Braiden had in mind.

Now, he'd invited her into his domain. Why? After the past couple days, that was the last thing she expected. His contrary behavior confused the heck out of her and her decision to be a part of his farm—the thought was still laughable—was leaning toward the positive. What did she have to lose?

*Plenty,* a voice whispered. Men like Angel, she knew, didn't do a damn thing without a good reason.

As she drove away from the garden courtyard of stores, it occurred to her that she was considering spending a couple of weeks with the man and she didn't know his last name.

Loaded down with more packages than any woman had a right to possess in one day, Calli's steps slowed as she neared her room, her face creasing with concern. The door was wide open and as she approached, fear skipped along her spine, tightening her muscles. She could hear voices. A police car, the door open, was parked beside her room. Radio noise crackled in the blistering heat. She set her bags down a few feet from the door and peered inside. She inhaled sharply.

Her room was ransacked. Everything—*everything*—was trashed. Her gaze shifted to the two police officers making notes and the hotel manager. The little Asian man was wringing his hands. Both officers turned to look at her, and the manager, Mr.

Wong, raced to her side, apologizing profusely. The maid had found the door open, he told her, and the room destroyed.

She looked to the officers.

And they looked back, one chubby and dark, the other blond.

"I'm the tenant," she said, her gaze scanning the debris of her suitcases and clothes. The mattresses were overturned, the drawers raped, but most of her clothes appeared intact. A man in a pale sport coat was dusting the place for fingerprints. One cop asked for ID and she went back for her bags, offering it to him.

"Who would do this? There wasn't much money in here." Not to do this kind of damage, she thought.

"Did you have anything of value? Cash? Documents? Jewelry?"

She nodded and moved to her cases, pulling them off the floor. She riffled in the compartments, sighing defeatedly, then held out a pair of diamond and ruby earrings, a gold bracelet and three rings. "All my cash, traveler's checks, bank card and two credit cards are gone." Damn, except for her checkbook and for the one credit card in her purse, she was broke. The officers exchanged a glance, then scribbled on their pads. "Everything else of value was with me, locked in my car."

The chubby officer nodded and wrote.

His partner, the blonde, tipped his hat back and looked at her at length. "Why would a woman who can afford Louis Vuitton luggage stay in a place like this?" He gestured to the plain, serviceable room.

"It's clean and cheap, the only hotel with room service and the luggage was a gift."

"But you drive a BMW."

"Your point?"

"That's a year's salary for some people."

"And I'll be paying on it till I'm eighty. Surely you have other questions besides the make of my car, which wasn't here at the time."

"We have to consider all possibilities of why they chose your room. Your car makes you a mark for a perp," he said, and she decided that was a reasonable explanation. He asked the time she left, if she locked up, who knew she was here, if she had any prescription medications, then he gestured to the manager. "Mr. Wong said there was a man with you the other night?"

Her gaze snapped to the manager and he flushed red. "Yes, but he wouldn't do this."

"How long have you known him?"

Calli bent to pick up her clothes off the floor, hastily stuffing her lacy lingerie back in the drawers. "We'd just met," she had to admit. One-night stand. She saw it plastered across their faces.

"I see. And his name?"

"Angel."

The blond officer looked at her expectantly, pen poised.

Her lips pressed into a tight line. "I don't know his last name."

"Griffin."

She and the officers turned toward the door. The hotel manager paled and mumbled something in his native tongue.

There he was, her personal bad penny, his shoulder braced on the cracked door frame, arms folded over his chest as if he'd just happened by. Damn, if Angel wasn't the most arrogant, infuriating man.

"Gabe," one officer said, smiling as he crossed the room, holding out his hand.

Calli moved to stand in front of Angel, folding her arms across her waist while the officer shook his hand. The officer was obviously surprised to see him. Interesting.

"Gabe, huh? And that's short for?" she urged, staring at him from beneath finely arched brows.

"Gabriel."

Angel. Gabriel. She let her gaze slid down his body and back up. "How...contrary."

His lips quirked. And her heart skipped an entire beat.

Gabe Griffin. Now, why did that sound familiar? Maybe she had heard one of the people in the bar call him that?

The officer glanced between them. "You know anything about this, Gabe?"

"Why would he?" Calli said in a taut voice. "He doesn't live here. Never stayed here." Her accusing gaze shot to the hotel manager.

"Miss Thornton has a tendency to run with the wrong crowd, Mike."

Her head snapped around, her blue gaze pinning like a blade. "Does that include you?" He was always in the right place at the right time, she thought, suspicious.

The officer smirked. "Knows you well enough, huh?"

"She thinks."

"Get out, *Gabriel*." She just wanted to knock that smug smile off his face. It had I-told-you-so written in every chiseled curve.

"I have to question him, ma'am."

"Do it on your own time, then. I want a copy of the report and I will let you know if anything else was stolen." She glanced at the room. "At this point, I'd say if they were looking for something more than money, it wasn't here."

The man dusting for prints closed up his case and Gabe was forced to step inside to let him pass.

"You mentioned things locked in your car. Would that be of interest?"

"I don't see how. Other than a gas credit card, a Visa and tip money in my purse, there's only my formula journal."

The officer's eyebrows lifted, his expression questioning.

Calli sighed. "I'm a chef. Executive chef for Excalibur Confections." Gabriel's brows rose into his forehead and she enjoyed the moment. She had the feeling there wasn't much that impressed him. "The journal contained my most recent recipes."

The officer's expression was condescending enough to infuriate her, but only another chef would know what that book was worth. It was why she kept it with her. But the fact that the officer didn't add it to his notes annoyed her. She rubbed her temple, a headache brewing. It was another half an hour before they left, and in that time Angel stood outside the door, talking softly with the officers. They all kept glancing at her as she called in her stolen traveler's checks and cards and returned the room to order. The hotel manager had a maid clean away the fingerprint dust and change the sheets, and he told her there would be no bill for her to pay. She smiled, assuring the little man that she wasn't going to sue because of his lack of security. He left, relieved.

"Ma'am," the blond officer said, stepping just inside. "I suggest you not stay here tonight. They might come back."

Her gaze shifted past him to Gabriel and his look dared her to rebel. She nodded and the police left.

Calli plopped down onto the edge of the freshly made bed and stared numbly out the window, a strange anger building in her. She felt violated and abused. Though nothing was ruined that she couldn't replace, she hated the sensation swimming in her veins. She wanted to beat the heck out of a punching bag for about an hour.

"Damn."

"This could have been because you've been seen with me." He was thinking of Tiny and Ike.

She looked up at the first words, her gaze narrowing. Pain sharpened in her head. "Are you saying *you* run with the wrong crowd, Mr. Griffin?"

He smirked, bracing his shoulders against the wall near the open door. "I've made a few enemies, and this week, so have you." Enough for someone to drug her one and only drink, he thought. And try to drag her into a limo.

She rolled her eyes. "Oh, please. This could have been random, and you know it."

"Do I?"

"Yes." But she didn't sound confident. How was she supposed to know who Gabriel Griffin, town bad boy, had ticked off lately? And what about Murdock? How did he fit in? She couldn't begin to wonder why she or her stuff was suddenly so important.

"There was more here to steal than cash," Gabe observed.

"But fencing it would bring attention. A quick turnover, isn't that what a thief wants?" Her eyes accused and he straightened.

"You think I did this?"

"No," she said, bowing her head. "No." There were too many other suspects; Murdock, Ike, Tiny, or some petty thieves who didn't know what they wanted.

Above her head, Gabe's face colored with guilt. If he'd had the chance, he would have done it just to get Daniel's private memo back. The fact that he was unscrupulous enough before he met her and that her mere presence redirected instincts he'd lived by, warned him enough to consider taking back his earlier offer.

But he didn't. It was reckless, he knew, and he moved to stand in front of her. She kept staring at her hands. He tucked up her chin till she met his gaze. His chiseled mouth tilted in a wry smile. "I told you so."

She jerked her chin from his grasp. "So you did." She hugged herself, glancing around her, and had the strange urge to shower. Calli wanted out of here. She was nearly broke till Monday, only a gas credit card and a Visa left, which was nearly maxed out till she could transfer some money on to the bill. And she'd already discovered that cashing a check in this town was like giving blood. The traveler's checks would be expressed to her on Monday at the least. She stared at her lap.

She could call Daniel, have him wire her pay, but pride kept her from that. Or she could go home. No, she thought, heading to the company suite in Acapulco and letting Excalibur Confections pamper her was the most logical solution.

She looked up.

She did have a choice.

Angel's.

Now *that was* dangerous.

And deep inside she wanted some. Mexico was easy. Being around Angel was not. She met his gaze and marshaled some courage to say the words, words that would cross the line between safe and sound...and hazardous...to her body and soul.

"Does your offer still hold?" The words stuck in her throat like dust. In her head, the nuns were screaming at her foolishness. But she wanted out of here and away from this place as soon as possible. It still felt like a crime scene.

He hesitated before answering. "Yeah, it holds."

"You don't sound so sure."

"Just wondering if you can handle it."

"Don't you mean, handle *you?*"

He held her gaze. "Scared?"

Now it was her turn to hesitate. "No."

He shrugged, noncommittal, and Calli had the feeling he was

smirking under that bland expression. Going with him was wild, reckless and maybe even stupid.

"I'll be ready in a few minutes."

Gabe nodded and tried not to show his relief that the totaled room was reason enough to push her to decide. Now if he could just figure out who'd done this. Murdock, who was a corporate raider, hadn't the time to do it himself, according to the sources Gabe had contacted after leaving Calli. But then, he didn't know the man's connections in this town or to Daniel that well. Yet. But the first thing Gabe was going to do when he spoke to Daniel was ream him for not telling him his "little ol' dessert company" was the infamous sword-in-the-sweet kind.

He observed her as she stood and stepped around the edge of the bed toward the dresser.

"Maybe you'll tell me how you got that nickname?" she said.

Gabe frowned. Her voice sounded strained.

"Calli?"

"Hmm?"

She was stuffing clothes into the cases with a speed that surprised him. She wouldn't look at him, gathering cosmetics from the bathroom, then dragging garments from the closet. But he caught her expression in the freshly cleaned closet mirror.

"Look at me."

She stopped and sighed, staring down at the garment bag. Slowly, she tipped her head back and met his gaze.

The haunted look in her eyes felt like a kick in the gut. "What's wrong?" he said in a soft voice.

She scoffed. "Like you'd understand." Her lower lip trembled, and briefly she caught it between her teeth.

As if approaching a wounded animal, he moved across the room. "You'd be surprised."

Her shoulders moved restlessly, then, after a few false starts, "I'm angry. Angry at myself for even coming here, at these people who felt justified," she said through gritted teeth, "to trash my room and touch my things." Her voice picked up volume and speed. "And I'm mad at you for being right, dammit!"

"You feel like you've been invaded, worked over as if someone beat you with a bat."

"Yes," she cried, sinking onto the mattress and staring at her hands.

Gabe kept a distance, propping his rear against the dresser and folding his arms, yet aching to wrap them around her. "Privacy isn't easy to keep, huh?"

"You know—" she tilted her head and glanced at him, then at nothing, her voice distant "—I tried for years to get some. When I was a kid it was always a line of beds, communal bathrooms, communal meals. Never an inch of space I could call my own." She laughed to herself, wiping at the tear moving down her cheek. "You should see my apartment, one person in a three-bedroom place. Sometimes I sleep in one of the empty rooms just because I can."

Gabe understood that. His own place was bigger than he needed and far enough away from neighbors that he didn't have to worry about an invasion. "I stayed in this house once that had twenty-seven people in it." She looked up at that and the words spilled from him without thought or hesitation. "Every hour of every day there were at least a dozen people in the living room, hungover, drunk, smoking something illegal, or just looking for a place to crash. We called it the 'House of What.'"

She frowned. "Why?"

"Because whenever anyone said something, everyone would look up, dazed and confused, and say 'Whaa?'" He made a sloppy, slack-jawed face and she smiled.

Well, he had a sense of humor.

"How long did you live there?"

"Never. I was one of those looking for a place to crash."

"Oh." What did she really know about this man? "Didn't you have a home?"

"No."

"That's it, just 'no'?" When he didn't respond she said, "I was raised in a Catholic orphanage."

His smile was barely there. "Figures."

"And you?"

He met her gaze and for the first time Calli saw raw emotion flicker there. It made her heart crack and bleed.

"Nowhere."

She took a step. "Angel?"

"Don't call me that!" came the bitter snap.

She reared back, her eyes wide. "Gabriel will take a little getting used to," she said softly, bravely moving closer. Oh, my, she thought, he has more wounds than she had a right to know. "Or do you prefer Gabe?"

Gabe wasn't going to admit that he liked hearing his name on her lips, that he'd actually thought about it enough to anticipate it. "Either is fine." He hesitated. "Just not Angel." It reminded him of an ugly time and he didn't want that part of him touching her. He pushed away from the dresser. "You ready?"

She looked suddenly nervous. "I suppose." She stood and shoved the garments into the bag, then zipped it shut.

"I hope you have some work clothes in there."

Her nose tipped the air. "Don't you worry about it." Then her brows knitted. "I won't be slopping pigs or anything like that, will I?"

"It's possible."

She made a face, then asked, "Are you going to pay me?"

"No."

She cocked her hip, her hand planted there. "Then what's the point?"

"Just keeping my enemies and whoever did this—" he nodded to the room "—away from you."

*Tough guy cares,* she thought with a hidden smile. "I'm getting the short end of the deal here."

His chiseled lips quivered with an almost smile. "Looks like it."

In that instant Calli realized she'd never seen him smile, not a full-blown, happy-to-be-alive smile. "You want a cook, don't you?"

He met her gaze. "Yes."

"I'm a chef, Gabriel."

It struck him, the sound of his name on her lips, sultry with a slight Southern drawl. It took a second to recover. "You haven't seen my kitchen."

She didn't like the sound of that. "Now that we're on the subject of requirements, I think we need a few rules."

He folded his arms and gave his full attention. The stance annoyed her. "And they are?"

"When we get to the farm—" She glanced to the side, then met his gaze, drawing a breath. "You cannot kiss me."

He arched a brow.

"No touching, either."

His face was blank and she wanted to pinch him. This was for her benefit, not his. Since she didn't feel she had *that* much of an effect on him, anyway.

"Absolutely no touching?" It was the way he said it that unnerved her, like a line drawn in the sand and a dare to cross it.

"None. If we're going to be living in the same house—" Oh, how the good sisters would give her an earful if they knew, she thought fleetingly. "We have to keep this impersonal."

"Agreed."

She sighed with relief. "I promise to do my share for room and board." She had to trade something in the bargain for her to feel she wasn't just using his place as a convenient getaway. "*If* I don't have to slop hogs. Roast them, yes. But meet them and stare into their beady little eyes before I sauté them, no thank you."

His lips were twitching and Calli realized her heart pounded with the anticipation of seeing him smile, just once. It didn't happen.

"Agreed."

She wished she could get more conversation out of him than those short abrupt sentences, she thought, but said, "Good. Fine."

Suddenly he stepped closer, his arm sliding smoothly around her waist and pulling her against his long body. The contact was electric, primal, and her hands flew to his chest.

"You agreed!"

Without a word, he ducked his head and covered her mouth with his, his kiss a slow slide of wet lips and tongue. And Calli responded and received, her heart racing up to her throat as her body softened and swelled and dampened with every move of his lips on hers. She didn't think there were any men left who kissed like this. Lush. Determined. A movie kiss. A tiny fraction of a moan came from him and then just as quickly, he pulled back.

"Gabriel!"

His lips curved a bit, his gaze sweeping her flushed face. "You said when we get to the farm—" He let the words hang between them as he released her and stepped back.

"I'm going to have to get this in writing I see," she muttered tightly, her lips numb and her body singing. Needing a separation, she swiftly collected up her shopping bags and walked out the door, heading to her car. She opened the trunk and he deposited her suitcase and garment bag inside. She topped it with her goodies.

"Where's your bike?"

"Didn't bring it." He nodded to a black truck parked at the far end of the lot. It was dented over the rear fender and covered in dust. "Just follow me," he said, pulling his keys from his pocket as he walked away. "And, Calli?"

She paused, one foot inside her car, one out.

Back-stepping, his gaze dropped briefly to her legs, then to her face. "The exit for the highway is about a mile down the road."

"I know."

"In case you decide to keep going."

His words were like a gauntlet dropped at her feet. A dare. And a way out. "You chicken?" she challenged. "Afraid I'll reform you or something?"

"No." His face was suddenly devoid of expression. "Afraid I'll corrupt you or something."

"You just try," she flung back. *Please.*

# Four

He'd lied.

It wasn't a farm, she decided as she left her car. Well, not really, and not at all what she expected. Yes, there were fields, though not large ones, but there was also a barn, a stable, a paddock and a corral. The latter penned three beautiful chestnut horses, playing tag from one end of the enclosure to the other. But it was the valley that took her breath away. Every shade of green and gold imaginable. It was as if a giant hand had scooped out a wide portion of tawny dry earth, making room for his ranch on a plateau between high, buff-colored walls. It made her feel insignificant just to look at it.

She loved it. It was solitude and silence and rich splashes of color in the wildflowers growing out of the stone cliffs, defying nature. Her heels sank into the dirt as she walked to a wide area serving as a driveway. Dust from the ride in swirled in a threat before settling. She gazed out over the land, hearing the gurgle of water over rocks, a horse stomping restlessly before scampering like a pleased child when Gabe moved close to the corral. She twisted to watch the animal nudge his hand and he stroked its long brown nose. Even in the distance she recognized the gentleness he kept hidden and she felt a sudden burst of jealousy.

For a horse?

Not the safest vein of thought, she warned herself, turning toward the one-level rambling house. Another surprise. Though it could use a coat of paint and some flowers around the porch supports, it was simple, serviceable. And the kitchen was...

"Outside?" she said, swinging around to look at him.

He pushed away from the fence, moving toward her. "Not up for the adventure?"

She ignored the sarcasm in his tone and said, "I can't picture you cooking here."

"I rarely cook anything, much less outside. Bull cooks."

"What or who is Bull?" Nothing pleasant came to mind.

"You'll know soon enough." She noticed he didn't come close to her, always several feet away.

"This Bull person isn't going to mind me invading his territory?"

"He'll be ecstatic."

Her brows tightened at the cryptic remark. He didn't offer an explanation. Typical. She looked at the kitchen. The entire area, including a wood dining table with six chairs and a long bench was protected by a porch stretching beyond the length of the house. The work area itself consisted of a water pump over a stainless-steel sink flanked by thick wood counters pressed up against the wall of the house. Opposite that and facing the open was a beautiful stone hearth with a grate for grilling. At least the view was spectacular, she thought as she approached, noticing a cove in the fitted stones to let bread rise. A three-by-five-foot table rested alongside the hearth, thick and smooth butcher block. She ran her hand over it like a caress. A chef's dream, she thought, the perfect height for herself. Her attention shifted to the *horno,* built far enough away from the house to not invite a fire hazard. She peered inside the blackened interior, then at him.

"Does this work?"

He nodded mutely and she felt his pale eyes follow her, intense as a touch.

Calli had never had to cook without electricity and she looked forward to the challenge. Especially the adobe oven that looked like a giant beehive. This will bake some incredible bread, she thought happily.

"Intimidated, I see."

He didn't know her well enough to recognize excitement when he saw it. She turned toward him, arms akimbo. "I suppose you will not only expect me to cook but be a ranch hand, too?"

Gabe sighed and raked his fingers through his hair, making it look wild. "Look, Calli. I don't expect anything from you." Her gaze sharpened on him. "I don't expect anything from anybody."

Me, either, she thought. "I agreed and I will. Or are you trying to get rid of me again?"

He hesitated and Calli thought he'd tell her he'd changed his mind about their arrangement. "Just making sure you understand."

She folded her arms and gave him her full attention. "Understand what, *exactly*?"

"That I didn't bring you here to get you into bed."

"What a shame," she muttered under her breath, looking at the ground.

"What?"

Her gaze flashed up, colliding with his. Self-preservation kicked in. He was not the tie-down-and-love-forever type. And she wasn't about to lose herself in a man that wouldn't give her what she needed. Not that she knew what that was. But sleep with him just because he had a sexy walk, a sexy voice and looked good with beard stubble? No way. "It would take a lot more than bringing me here to get me into your bed, Gabriel."

Gabriel. God, he liked the way she said his name, a slight Southern drawl, aristocratically soft. But her words sounded too much like a threat and something, he wasn't sure what, broke inside him. *You're not good enough for her anyway, man. So just back off.* She's a case, an assignment. And if he kept thinking of her that way he just might live through the next couple of weeks. Yet like Adam tempted by Eve, he let his gaze wander over her lemon-yellow dress, the matching heels dusted with dirt. His body tightened from just looking at her and he was a little glad she'd started rooting in the cabinets.

"Pitiful." She tsk-tsked.

"You're really going to cook?" Damn, if he didn't sound like an eager kid.

Bent to look in a lower cupboard, she turned her head and flashed him a smile. "It's what I do best."

Not really, he thought, but he hadn't tasted her cooking, only her kisses. Jeez, he needed to get away from her. Striding to her car, he released the trunk latch from inside and retrieved her luggage.

"I can do that," she said as he passed into the house.

He ignored her and she hustled in after him. The inside was as plain as the outside. And dreary. She stood in the entry, her gaze passing over the beige stuffed chairs and sofa, the chair with a permanent dent in the seat from his body. There was nothing special, nothing personal, about the place. Even the southwest design seemed to lack the style's usual appeal. His boot heels sounded in the hall off to the left corner and she walked toward the noise. She passed a closed door, a bathroom with a claw-footed tub, then headed to a room at the back. He was setting her bags on the floor as she stepped through the door.

He hooked his thumbs in his pockets and stepped back from her. "There are two others if you don't like this one."

She'd noticed the doors farther up the hall. "This is fine." *And which is your room?* she wanted to ask. *And why am I really here, Gabriel? Did you really need free labor that bad?* She didn't think so.

Her own reasons were clear. It was totally and utterly reckless. Gabriel Griffin was bad company, raw seduction in tight jeans, and even with the rules she'd set down, the good sisters' warnings played in her head. She ignored them, feeling like Eve in the garden of temptation. What was it going to be like, living with a man that threw her hormones out of whack whenever he looked at her? Like he was doing to her now. Her body senses were heightened, aware of even his breathing, and she quickly focused on the simply decorated room, spared of clutter. A tall dresser, nightstands flanking the double bed, both with squat oil lamps, and a beautiful handmade quilt spread across the bed. There were a couple of terra-cotta urns and pots on the floor and dresser, all without flowers or plants. The furniture had an unstained rough quality, like frontier antiques. A rag rug in sandy tones covered the floor. Not bad for a guy's place, she thought.

When she didn't respond, he started to leave.

"It's nice, Gabriel." She turned her head and met his gaze as he twisted a look over his shoulder. "So, what is it that you do out here, all alone?"

"I train horses for trail riding."

He looked anxious to leave. And she didn't want him to just yet. "I didn't know they had to be trained."

His hot gaze slid over her. "The animals aren't bred to be ridden, Cal."

She felt heat warm her cheeks and tilted her chin defiantly. His low tone reeked of sexual innuendo. "I'm sure I'll learn a lot while I'm here." She moved to her suitcases, dragging one onto the bed and sending the zipper around. She flipped the top back, then glanced at him. His gaze seemed to scrap over her.

"Are you planning to watch me change?"

He smirked, but his mind's eye was peeling away the feminine layers faster than she could ever imagine. "Make yourself at home. Need anything, just ask. I'll be in the barn."

Calli let her breath out, then shut the door after him. Quickly, she stripped out of her dress and heels and into an old pair of cutoffs and a tank top. She dug into the bottom of the suitcase for sneakers and socks, not about to opt for sandals on a ranch. She was going to investigate this place first, then report for *duty*. A smile stretched her lips. *Angel, honey,* she thought, *don't think for a minute that I can't hack it.* She would die before admitting she didn't know a thing about ranching. Or handling him.

Leaving the room, she snooped and found he liked books. There were shelves lining the walls on either side of the living room fireplace, stacks of them under the end tables. Even two or three with places marked. His taste held a wide variety from Asimov to Clancy.

Avoiding the rooms with the doors closed, she investigated the bathroom next. Finding the flushing toilet was like manna from heaven, until she realized that if she wanted a bath, she had to haul water from outside. Ten minutes later, she amended the idea when she found an outdoor shower. With slats of polished, treated wood and a pull chain to operate the flow of water, it looked more like a sauna. She shook her head, amused. Water, obviously heated by the sun, was stored in a tank on stilts with God knew what else lurking in its depths. This, she thought, was roughing it. What's a few inconveniences? She could have said no, she reminded herself, and he did warn her.

*Not up for the adventure?*

Was he daring her to stay or daring her to fold and leave?

That there was a generator, humming like an old man trudging uphill, told her he didn't do without as much as he would like her to believe. Following the lines, she found they ran to the refrigerator standing on the porch/kitchen and to a washer. At least I won't be beating my clothes against a rock, she thought.

She walked around the yard, the field, stooping to pick herbs from the overgrown garden. Someone had made an effort once and the rows of herbs hidden in weeds were halfway decent. It was the second thing on her mental list. Food was the first.

She rummaged in the cabinets, the fridge, and found enough staples to make a meal. But that was it. Well, she would ask him to point her in the direction of the nearest store later. Her inventory limited, she managed a surprise, then went searching for Gabe. And she found him.

Oh, Hail Mary, did she find him.

He was in the barn, stripped to the waist and shoveling dung into a wheelbarrow. The barn was cool and dry, the odor palatable after a few seconds, but that hardly mattered to the option of watching Gabe in rancher mode. She swallowed, wetting her lips as he bent and scooped and tossed. A horse watched him as if this were a lesson he had to learn, and Calli simply watched, learning a lot in the few seconds. His body was carved marble, thick arms and shoulders, a trim, flat waist, and every inch she could see was bronze. She wanted to touch him. Bad.

"Gonna burn a hole into my back or what?"

Startled by the annoyance in his voice, she straightened. "Well, if you're going to take that kind of attitude, I won't give you this." He turned, propping his arm on the top of the handle, his gaze traveling over her attire with slow approval. She felt im-

mediately hotter under his velvety gaze and held out a tall glass
of lemonade. He let go of the shovel, snatching a raggedy towel
off a peg as he moved toward her, wiping the sweat from his face
and chest. *Oh, don't,* she thought, *I like the sweat.* It looked good,
trickling down the center of his bare chest, his temples, mingling
with bits of hay in his dark hair. But what startled her the most
were the tattoos on his arms.

Nowhere else, but his arms. A ring of thorns around one bicep;
a Tasmanian Devil in a dust cloud on the other. A dragon-
wrapped dagger pointed down on one forearm to where Celtic
knots circled his wrist. Turquoise and yellow flames shot up from
the other and curled around his elbow, and USMC labeled one
deltoid. Then she noticed something else. The scars. One in his
side, jagged and shiny, a slice under his stubbled chin, and a deep
gouge on his left shoulder that looked like a—

"Is that a bullet hole?"

He took the glass. "Yeah." Tipping it to his lips, his Adam's
apple climbed and fell as he drained it. He wiped the back of his
hand across his mouth, his pale gaze colliding with hers as he
handed it back. "Where did you find lemons?"

Go ahead, avoid telling me your secrets, she thought peevishly.
"The fridge, though most of them could have walked away on
their own."

His lips curved, then receded. "Need to shop?"

"Every woman needs to shop, Gabriel. But as to food, yes, if
you want to eat tomorrow."

Gabe wanted to eat, all right, but she was on his menu. If he
thought she looked hot in leather or that simple yellow dress,
nothing prepared him for very short cutoffs and a body-fitting,
hot-pink tank top. She had the best-looking legs he'd ever seen
on a woman and his imagination saw him licking every inch of
those defined muscles. He wondered what she did to get them to
look like that and in the same instance knew he should be thinking
of her as an employee. Except he wasn't paying her and she didn't
look like a ranch hand.

"Need help? Or are there hogs to slop?"

"No hogs."

Her lips tightened. "I didn't think so."

"Just chickens." He inclined his head to the coop a hundred feet or so away from the barn. "And they're taken care of."

"I can shovel hay," she offered.

"Not opting for horse turds?"

"When you look like the expert?" She shook her head. "Ain't no way."

He smirked, then turned away without a word and picked up the shovel. She stood there, watching.

The silence stretched and when he spoke, his voice was heavy with impatience. "Go back to the house, Calli."

His tone stung. "You're welcome, *Angel*," she snapped. She headed out, head bowed, arms folded over her waist, when the sound of a vehicle approaching brought her head up. She stopped short. Gabe was right behind her as a truck, old and faded red, jostled and bounced up the road in a cloud of dust.

"That'll be Bull."

"I'm thrilled," she said over her shoulder, her gaze thin with hurt. He was oblivious and she quickened her steps toward the house. Gabe couldn't keep his gaze from her sweet little bottom shifting inside the short shorts, teasing him with the soft curves shaped in frayed cloth. Sweet.

The truck skidded to a halt and Gabe strode to the man leaving the vehicle. Bull was big, barrel-chested, with heavy short legs. Gray hair stuck out in all directions from beneath a beat-up, stained straw cowboy hat, which was curved to perfection, as Bull would say. He wore worn jeans and a T-shirt ringed at the neck with sweat. His daily attire. Usually his shirts said something across the chest. Today it was washed-out blue with Runs With Scissors printed across the front.

"You steal that, boss?" Bull asked, his eyes twinkling as he nodded to the BMW.

"It belongs to her." Gabe didn't point and waited until Bull's pale blue gaze searched the ranch for a human life.

His eyes widened and he whistled softly. "Damn, son. You act like a hermit for years and bring a woman like *that* here?" Bull grinned, his gaze still lingering on Calli as she stooped to arrange wood in the hearth. Gabe explained why she was here.

"Aw, now who would want to hurt her? She's just a little thing.

Hell, a good wind'd take her clean to the river. Damn, but she's a cute one, ain't she?" He glanced at Gabe.

"Yeah. Cute." Gabe wasn't looking at her. It might give too much away when he did and Bull was good for latching on to the tiniest thing and running with it. He decided to redirect his attention. "She's a chef."

Bull's eyes narrowed. "What'd you mean?"

"An-honest-to-God, card-carrying chef. Culinary school, degreed, specializes in pastries." Was that pride he heard in his own voice?

"No kidding?"

"Best of all, she's agreed to cook." Gabe waited for a reaction.

"Thank God," he moaned. "One less chore I don't need." Bull eyed him. "How'd you manage that?"

"It was either that or let her slop hogs."

Bull frowned. "We ain't got no hogs."

"She knows. Now."

Bull chuckled softly, removing his hat and scraping his hair back over across his head, then repositioning the hat. Gabe ducked into the barn and grabbed his shirt off a nail, noticing that Bull tucked his own into the back of his trousers as he neared her.

She looked up, smiling, her gaze on the man beside Gabe as she moved around the hearth, her hand out. Gabe introduced them and Bull dragged the hat from his head, smoothed his hair again and ducked his head. His cheeks were red and Gabe didn't think he'd ever seen him this shy.

"I'm sure glad you're doing this." Bull waved to the outdoor kitchen.

"My pleasure, Mr. Pierce."

"The name's Harlan."

"No wonder you never told me," Gabe snickered, working his shirt on over damp skin.

Calli sent him a shut-up-before-I-kick-you look and smiled at Bull. "I take it these—" she gestured to the upper cabinets with locks "—are to keep out animals?"

"Yes, ma'am. There's a passel more just in there." He pointed to a side door, then moved around the hearth to show her the pantry just inside the house. "I know it ain't what yer likely used to—"

"I'm sure I can manage. Hungry?"

Bull beamed. Gabe arched a dark brow. Calli ignored him. If he was going to be bossy and impolite, she would rise above it. Besides, she'd yet to figure out what she'd done to deserve his rudeness. "If you'll give me about twenty, thirty minutes..." She let that hang and at least Bull was wise enough to understand that she didn't want company while she prepared. Gabe wasn't getting the hint.

She pulled out pots and pans, then removed the grate over the hearth and stacked in wood. She tossed in a lit match. It didn't catch. She was nervous as he stood there watching her light one long kitchen match after another.

"Kindling," he finally said, and she looked up. "Like a tee-pee." He shaped a model with his hands.

"Would have helped five matches ago," she muttered, and squatted to make a proper fire. She blew on the smoky flames, adding piece after piece of splintered wood. It caught nicely and she straightened, coaxing a good blaze. Charcoal would be easier and she would buy some when she went for supplies. After cleaning the grate, she replaced it and gave him her back as she pumped water into a pan. She set it on the fire to boil, then rooted in the cabinets. He was still there. She could feel his eyes on her.

"Go back to the barn, Angel."

His lips tightened. "Don't call me that."

She glanced at him over her shoulder. "Then go back to the barn, *Gabriel*." She placed spices on the counter, set out a sack of rice, then straightened and grabbed a bowl, heading toward the small overgrown garden.

Gabe understood instantly. "There's snakes in there."

She stopped short, then marched over to a pile of kindling and picked up a long stick. "I'll scream before I keel over and die," she assured him with a tight glance, then she stirred the ground, hoping to evict anything that liked ankles for lunch. Calli felt perspiration bead between her breasts and her shoulder blades, more from him watching her than the heat. He did that a lot, stared without saying a word, and she was relieved when she heard his boots crunching against the dirt as he headed back to the barn.

Calli poked at the ground, deciding she would ask Bull to check for snakes next time. Squatting, she sifted through weeds for fresh herbs, reminding herself that the men were hungry and she'd no time to play Martha Stewart and do some weeding. She smiled to herself and wondered if they would eat what she had planned. Anything would be better than the refried beans and tortillas, all of which she had found in abundance. Of course, after smelling horse turds all day, *he* ought to be grateful for water.

Gabe pushed the wheelbarrow up the truck ramp and dumped the aromatic contents into the flatbed, then returned for more. There always seemed to be more work than time and he wondered at his decision to start this place. It didn't look much different than the day he'd bought it two years ago. He shoved and hauled, then swept before he broke open a hay bale, spearing and spreading. His clothes were soaked with sweat, but not a bit of work stopped him from watching her. She was at the table, the long knife moving with a speed that defied logic. Pots steamed and a fragrance that was close to flowers, scented the air. He didn't know where she found anything decent, but it sure smelled good. And he was starving by the time she rang the bell. Gabe forced himself not to bolt like a kid and took his time washing up, then following Bull, who was walking faster than he'd seen in months.

"It's cooler inside," she said, inclining her head toward the door, her hands full of plates. Bull leaped forward and opened the screen door and Gabe almost smiled. The old man ought to start drooling any second.

Following them, Gabe stopped short at the sight of his table, in his house. Didn't look like anything he remembered. She'd used an old runner for a tablecloth, the heavy Mexican-style stripes making the whole room bright. But it was the table setting that caught him off guard. The dishes and glassware had come with the place. Gabe had found the box, but never used them, both he and Bull making use of the disposable kind. Tall, slim glasses sparkled, flatware gleamed and a bouquet of wildflowers in a cracked pot made him smile inside. He felt like a creep for being rude to her. No one had ever done anything like this for him. Ever. And like the lemonade she'd brought when he was dying of thirst, Gabe couldn't remember the last time someone had thought of his comfort. He didn't want to like it. And he sure as hell didn't want to need it.

She set the last plate on the table and stepped back to inspect. "I know it might not be what you're used to, but I had to improvise."

She was right, Gabe thought, glancing over the abundance of food. This was nothing like he was used to. Nothing. Jeez. It looked like a restaurant.

"After lunch I'll take a trip to town for supplies." Her tone implied that she would go alone. Gabe had other ideas. And staring down at her, her body damp from the heat, her hair a little mussed, he had other ideas that had zilch to do with buying groceries.

She gestured and they sat, helping themselves.

Calli bit the inside of her mouth and waited for a reaction to the rice flavored with spices and seasoned with flowers and herbs, grilled beef strips and wild onions with peppercorns and cumin. Fresh basil and lemon helped make the canned peas palatable. A quick-brewed tea was iced and sweetened with crushed mint and she rose to pour them each a glass. She didn't have time for a dessert, a must in her book—and would make up for it later.

Calli ate sparingly, sipped tea and watched them. Bull had no trouble with devouring everything in front of him, yet Gabe was another matter. He tasted each dish, carefully.

"Calli?"

"Hmm?" She'd been waiting for this. His chewing had slowed, his frown more curious than mad.

"What am I eating?" He pushed the pink blossoms to the edge of his plate.

"Flowers."

He spat it out in his napkin.

"Oh, come on, you were enjoying it just fine until I told you." His look said he didn't care, he wasn't eating flowers.

"Trust me, they're edible." She looked pointedly at Bull, who was already scraping the remains of his food to the edge of the plate for the final bite. "And you eat herbs, don't you?" No response. "Half of the herbs are flowers." His expression was impassive. "Think I'm trying to poison you?"

Bull looked up, the fork halfway to his mouth. He stared at Calli, then Gabe, then must have decided she was trustworthy, or that he'd come this far, and shoved the food into his mouth. Calli's smile was smug as she propped her arms on the table, her chin on her fists and looked directly at Gabe.

And he looked back. He couldn't get enough of those blue eyes, that energetic smile. She was so pretty and bubbly and he wanted some of that. But knew he couldn't, so he savored just looking at her. He scooped up a spoonful of flowers and ate them. Damn, if she wasn't right.

Then she smiled.

And Gabe thought the sky had opened up.

Lord, this was going to be pure hell living with her.

"You gonna eat that?" Gabe's glance slid to Bull, who was eyeing Gabe's unfinished lunch.

Gabe hid a smile. "I'd planned on it."

Bull's expression wilted.

"There's plenty." She moved the bowls and platters in front of him. He eyed the helpings, then her.

"Go on, Bull, I've finished." She sighed. "Wish I had dessert, though."

They both looked disappointed.

"I promise tomorrow it will be something special."

It was another ten minutes of silence while the men ate, cleaning the platters.

"Heck, Miss Calli," Bull said, wiping a napkin across his mouth. "That there was the best. The best." Bull sat back in his chair and drained the rest of his iced tea.

She nodded and smiled, then her gaze shifted to Gabe's.

She didn't need to hear his reaction.

She knew it. Her heart leaped.

Then she told herself she shouldn't be so thrilled that she'd passed muster.

Gabe swallowed, his gaze moving intensely over her. "Proved you're not all pastries with little swords in them, didn't you?"

It sounded like a challenge, even to his own ears, yet she beamed. His heart skated to his throat at the sight of it.

"You doubted, admit it."

"You're hired," he said as if it killed him.

Her eyes flashed wide. "Hired? Does that mean you're going to actually *pay* me?"

He frowned. "Room and board, sure."

A purely feminine smile graced her face, mischievous and downright seductive. Bull glanced between the two, then stood, left the table, then the house, whistling.

The screen door slammed behind him. Then silence.

"That's all?"

She had no idea what that look was asking or even implying, he thought. Why would someone as beautiful and wealthy enough to do what she wanted, be with whomever she desired, want anything to do with him? He was nothing. And in his wildest dreams, he wouldn't be good enough or clean enough for a woman like Calli Thornton.

And if she knew how he'd lived, what he'd done to reach thirty, she would be running for that expensive car and peeling rubber for a mile.

Her nightmares were his reality.

She might be safe from Murdock here, but she wasn't safe from him. He shoved back the chair and stood. "You made the rules and a deal's a deal." He headed for the door.

"Gabriel?" He paused on the threshold, his back to her. It shouldn't feel so good to hear her call his name, he thought, and the vulnerability made him angry. "Gabe?"

He snapped a look back over his shoulder.

"I was teasing."

Teasing? Didn't she realize what just the *thought* of touching her did to him? "Don't," he warned, trying to make her understand who he really was. "Because I could take your body on that table and walk away, Calli. Easy." His tone and words intentional, shoving the memory of the last night in her face.

Her features tightened. "Is implying that you've done that, on this table, supposed to scare me?"

Her defiant tone said she wouldn't let it go and Gabe crossed to her, dragging her from the chair and up against him. He bent her back till their bodies meshed. The hot contact drove desire up his spine. He grew instantly hard. And that he couldn't have her, couldn't lose himself in her sweet innocence, made him ache. And angrier.

"Don't play games with me, Calli. Ever. I've taken women in the back seats of cars, on the floor, the desert and in broad daylight for the world to see. So don't think for a second what you've got—" his icy gaze raked her "—is something I haven't had."

Abruptly, he released her and left the house, his stride long and pounding. And if he thought he'd left her shaken and hurt, he was wrong.

He knew it the instant the onion hit him in the back of the head.

# Five

Gabe stopped, the onion bouncing to the ground and rolling a few inches beyond his feet. He stared at it for a second, then cocked a look back over his shoulder, rubbing his neck.

Calli stared back, feeling very unattractive right now. *Don't think for a second what you've got is something I haven't had.* "I don't need to know what a slut you were, Gabriel."

His brows shot up and he faced her, hooking his thumbs in his belt loops, hips slanted. "Is that a way for a good Catholic girl to talk?" He was strangely pleased that she'd face up to him like this.

"You wouldn't know a good girl," she said, tossing another onion like a baseball, "if she were right in front of you."

He moved slowly toward her, his gaze traveling hotly over her body like a predator to his prey. And Calli knew it was absolute rebellion that kept her rooted to the floor, her gaze locked with his. She felt more for this man than any other, ever, and if he could ignore the sexual attraction, then so could she.

He stopped inches from her, viewing her from his height, and she craned her neck to look up at him. "Yes. I do."

It was her turn to smirk. "Don't assume you know anything about me, Gabriel, and I'll do the same for you. And if you had any respect for me, beyond my culinary talents, you wouldn't have talked to me that way."

"I do respect you."

The sincerity of his tone startled her. She frowned. Was he throwing his past in her face to prove he was too jaded for even pleasant conversation with a woman raised by nuns? He couldn't know his past would never matter to her. No one's did or she would never have hired Rodrigez for Excalibur. Oh, there was more to Gabriel Griffin than the dangerous-to-body-and-soul image he projected, all right. And he didn't want anyone to know it. Or see beyond it.

"If that's true, then you owe me an apology."

"For the truth?" He couldn't; it was who he was. Nothing.

"No." She shoved him back. "For the way you said it."

She didn't wait for the words and turned into the house, tossing the onion once before dropping it into a bowl. She collected up dishes, aware he was still there, staring. He couldn't get within ten feet of her without her body calling out like a whistle siren. She fought the urge to turn to look at him.

Gabe stared at her back and wanted to go to her, slide his arms around her and say the words she wanted to hear. But they weren't in him to say. It bothered him that she cared, that she needed to hear *him* apologize. He didn't want the responsibility of her heart.

This was temporary anyway, he reminded himself. And he was getting too caught up in her, as if there would be a tomorrow. And even if he let go of everything holding him back and indulged in her, he would destroy her, like he'd done everything gentle in his life. She didn't want to know him. Not really. She was just curious. But a part of him dared to reveal the ugliness, wanted her to know the things he'd done to survive. *Then she'll run,* a voice whispered. But the worst of it, beyond the sheer ungodly temptation of Calli, was the niggling doubt that even after she knew, she would stay.

Calli sighed deflatedly when she heard him walk away. She finished collecting up the dishes into an old basket she'd found, seeing as there was nothing left of the meal to discard, then carried them outside to the sink. She pumped water into a clean pan, setting it on the grill to heat, then went back to the sink to wash dishes. Beneath the shade of the porch, she scrubbed, determined to keep to herself. Not that *that* would be much fun. She cast a look over her shoulder, the sponge clutched in her hand. He was in the paddock, walking a pregnant horse around the ring. Damn. That line in the sand was growing wider, she thought, tempting her to risk her heart and leap the chasm.

An hour later Gabe crossed the yard to the kitchen, pumped water into a glass and tipped it to his lips. He stopped mid-drink, his gaze narrowing. She was in the garden, pulling weeds, but it just wasn't that that grabbed his full attention, but her position, on her knees, her sweet behind in the air as she leaned out to pluck and dig. The back of her tank top was soaked dark with sweat, her legs sparkled with it. He finished the drink, set the glass aside and strode toward her. He knew he shouldn't, should go back to work. But like an addict, he needed a fix. Of her. As he neared, he noticed she wore a baseball cap and her knees were braced on a couple of dish towels. She was collecting the weeds into a bucket. She didn't acknowledge him, but he knew she'd heard him. And it irritated him.

Until he heard a faint tinny sound and realized she was listening to music through headphones. Her bottom bounced, her shoulders shifting, and she sang out, plucking weeds in time to the music. His lips curved and he simply watched her. He'd never seen anyone have so much fun working in this unbearable heat. And in that instant, he wanted her to notice him. Yet when she stood, twisting to work a kink out of her back, then pick up a hoe, he decided it could wait. She danced between the neat rows of herbs and flowers, digging the hoe in time to whatever music that was blaring in her head. What kind was it? His curiosity aroused, Gabe realized he wanted to know more about her than he needed to get the job done.

He had been hired to protect her.

Not want her so bad he could taste it.

Still, he watched her compact body shifting, her hips rocking, and she used the handle of the hoe like a partner, sort of, straddling the upright stick and dirty dancing her way down to a squat to pick at some more weeds. Gabe found himself envying a stick of wood. It wasn't until she whirled around for the big finish that she saw him.

She froze, nearly tripping over her feet, then blinked. And even in the bright New Mexico sun he could see a blush steal into her face.

"Enjoying yourself?"

She switched off the music and stared. "What?" she said, more curious than impatient.

He didn't respond, his gaze moving over her sweat-glistened skin, the trickles moving down her temples, along her throat to disappear between her breasts. He remembered the sweet taste of her skin.

"Gonna get sunburned."

She pulled off her hat and the headset, then fluffed her hair. It was soaked, too. "Is that why you came over here? To tell me to protect my skin?"

Was she still expecting an apology? Though her tone told him more than he wanted to know, another clue came by the way she was holding the hoe, as if she wanted to wrap it around his neck. And why the hell had he come over? He wasn't about to tell her that her body was like a magnet as much as her untouchable energy. But he'd felt like a teenager not invited to the party that was going on right next door. He'd just wanted a look, as if seeing what he couldn't have would make him feel any better. Masochist, he thought bitterly.

"You check for snakes?" He nodded to the ground around her feet.

"Yes, there were a few," she lied baldly. "But after introductions we've come to a compromise. I won't smash them with the hoe and they agreed not to bite me."

He smirked. "Just be careful. The nearest hospital is forty miles away."

She nodded. He stared, searching her delicate features and craving a taste of her. He clenched his fists to keep from taking what he wanted. Absently, she pulled her shirt from her shorts and wiped at the sweat on her chest. Gabe's eyes flared as she twisted the fabric in a knot beneath her breasts. Her stomach was tanned and contoured and he wondered what she looked like in a bikini, then his imagination took off in a dead run and he wondered what she looked like naked.

Oh, sweet mercy, Calli thought. Those pale eyes might lack emotion sometimes, but when they didn't, they had the ability to liquify her insides. She felt stripped and appraised. She could do no more than stare back and tell herself she *had* to ignore the attraction between them. Her body warned her that it was next to impossible, animalistic desire running through her blood. And she wished she could read him better. It was just a look, she thought, and forced herself to remember each syllable he'd spouted at her at lunch. Inasmuch as Gabriel Griffin was pure erotic temptation, Calli's feelings were smarting.

Then he tipped his head to one side, sunlight dancing off the tiny gold loop in his ear. It forced reality ahead of desire. As did the tattoos disappearing in the darkness of his tan and the scars marking him with the brutality of his unknown past. They might have had disadvantages in their lives, but they were still from different worlds. Desire could take a person only so far. And a woman didn't get involved with a man like Gabriel Griffin, a man so unapproachable, and not go in with both feet and damn the consequences.

And she wasn't prepared to risk a thing for him.

Not until he saw beyond the *good girl.* No, she needed to stay clear of him.

"Protect my skin, check for snakes. Was there anything else?" Her expression was bland, her tone implying that he should either apologize for his previous behavior or leave her alone.

When he didn't respond, she had her answer. She wasn't worth an apology. Calli didn't watch him go and immediately replaced the ball cap and headphones. She switched on her tape player, ignoring the wild pounding in her heart from just being near him.

"Dammit, Daniel, I ought to beat the stuffing out of you," Gabe snarled into the cellular phone five minutes later. "Why didn't you tell me your company was Excalibur?'' Gabe peered around the edge of the barn to be certain Calli was still in the garden.

"Hello, Gabriel," came dryly through the phone. "And why should it matter?"

Because Gabe hadn't seen Daniel in years and the last time had been when Gabe was caught burglarizing Daniel's house in a posh section of New Mexico, not fifteen miles from here. Daniel had given him a break: a man to call for a real job. Gabe had taken it and never looked back. He owed him. And when he peered for another look at the woman in his garden, he knew that paying up was costing him more than he had to give.

Gabe told him about Murdock and the break-in. Daniel cursed, spouting his regret. Gabe didn't have any sympathy.

Bull passed him carrying a bucket of oats, not sparing Gabe a glance as he leaned against the barn wall and talked into the cigarette-pack-size phone.

"Details, pal. Now. I need to know everything."

Daniel was protecting her from a corporate spy who he insisted was trying to steal a copy of Excalibur's winter line of desserts. For which Calli had the only copies. Which was why he'd pan-icked when she hadn't shown up at the company suites in Aca-pulco. The memo detailed a suspected scheme to bootleg copies of Excalibur Confections with cheap ingredients, and it would destroy the company financially, not to mention its reputation. And Calli's. And Daniel wanted the memo back before Calli could get involved. She'd accidentally picked it up off his desk with her files and by the time Daniel had figured out where it went, Calli had left.

"Did you get it?"

"It's a little hard to search when her briefcase and journal are with her all the time, and if she realizes her stuff's been raked over, guess who's the prime suspect?" He didn't want to think of how she would react to that.

"Listen, Gabe," Daniel said tiredly. Gabe could hear the frus-tration and concern in his voice. "Just keep her and that journal together. I'll do the rest. Calli doesn't know she has the memo, so we have nothing to worry about now."

"She isn't stupid."

"I know that!"

"I don't like this."

"Getting a conscience?"

*Yes.* "Screw you."

"Look. If she knew that memo named one of her chefs as Murdock's co-conspirator, it would destroy her and she'd be on the first plane back here to confront him. I need to get to the bottom of this first. She hired him and she'd feel responsible and betrayed."

More than if she discovered exactly why she was living in his house? he wondered, Or why they'd met in the first place? A stab of unaccustomed guilt lanced through him and he closed his eyes, leaning his head back against the painted wall.

"But you have to get it back."

"I will. In my own time."

Gabe cut the line without saying goodbye, then collapsed the phone and shoved it into his back pocket. The sooner he got that lousy piece of paper, the sooner Calli would be out of his world. Pushing away from the wall, he walked around the edge of the barn and reached for the broom propped against the west wall. His hand stilled, and from the distance, his gaze greedily raked her like a man starved for the sight. *Do you really want her gone, man?* As if she felt his stare, she straightened, twisting and arching her arm over her head to block the sun. She stared back. And after a second or two, she smiled slightly. Gabe snatched up the broom, turned on his heels and went to sweep out a stall. He wondered which was worse. Keeping her from discovering someone wanted her journal more than her or that not only had one of her trusted chefs betrayed her, eventually Gabe would, too. Then he decided anything he did wouldn't matter to her.

But he wanted it to.

Gabe was out of the barn and leaping the fence just as she peeled down the driveway, the wheels of her car spitting pebbles and dust. She was leaving him. Then he corrected himself. There was no *them.* Never would be, and again, it ticked him off. He called to her, but she didn't stop and he immediately rushed to his bike, turning over the engine and following her. Damn woman. What the hell was she thinking? Then it occurred to him that she didn't know someone wanted to hurt her for those damn recipes. He maneuvered the bike behind her, then alongside, keeping up with the BMW on the narrow, barren rode. He tapped the glass. She didn't look at him.

"Dammit, Calli, pull over!"

She stopped abruptly, fishtailing the car, and threw the gear into park.

He wiped his face across his T-shirt sleeve and waited for her to send the electronic window down.

"Is there a problem?" she asked blandly.

His eyes narrowed and he caught the bite to her tone. *That's my fault,* he thought.

"Don't leave this ranch without me, Calli."

"Why?"

"The break-in and Murdock good enough reason? Not to mention, I have enemies."

She rolled her eyes. "I'm a big girl. I've taken care of myself for a long time, bad boy, and you made it rather clear that I am meaningless to you other than my ability to sauté and simmer."

He looked away then, staring out over the canyon, and Calli was again arrested by his harsh profile, his eyes, a pale green devoid of emotion. *He hides everything too well,* she lamented silently.

His fingers flexed on the handlebars. "Running away?" he said softly, then looked at her.

"Don't flatter yourself, *Angel.*" His eyes narrowed sharply. "And I didn't need you to go with me to grocery shop." Was that relief she saw in his expression?

"Nowhere without me. Clear?"

Calli let her gaze travel over his, liking his protectiveness and the way his black T-shirt hugged his chest and arms. She inclined her head. "Come on then."

He turned off the bike and sent the kickstand down, taking the key and leaving the cycle where it was. He snatched up his jacket where it was thrown across the seat, then slid into the car and slammed the door. She took off like a jackrabbit and he glared at her.

"I thought you were broke?" Not that he would let her buy his groceries anyway, but he was curious.

"I was going to see if I could write a check."

So. She did have access to some money at least. And that meant she wasn't here because she had nowhere else to go. He wondered why she'd come with him, exactly. Hell, he could follow her again and she'd never know it. That she chose his place confused him. Of course, he'd baited her into coming here just so he could keep a close eye on her the easy way. But he never understood *her* reasons. Who would want to cook for ranch hands when she could be in Acapulco, relaxing in the sun?

He didn't like being this curious about her.

He didn't like it at all.

She shifted gears and drove faster.

"You're speeding."

She eased her foot off the gas and coasted, then resumed.

"You're staring."

Gabe couldn't help it. It was obvious she'd bathed and changed, her hair still damp at her nape and held back with a headband. She wore a cropped black top and her lime-green shorts showed off her tanned legs.

"Liked the outdoor shower?"

Okay, Calli thought. If that was the safest subject he could come up with, she would play. "You built that, didn't you?" His brows shot up. "I knew it," she said smugly. "I was amazed that the water was so warm."

"So was I, the first time." An image flashed in her mind, Gabe in the shower, sudsy and lean and...she had to stop thinking like that.

She gave him a small smile, banishing her imagination. He seemed to relax a little and when they hit town, he gestured to the parking lot on the right. Calli drove into a slot and was out of the car and walking to the entrance before she realized he wasn't with her.

She faced him. His rear braced on the trunk, he looked as

belligerent as a schoolboy. The image would have worked, if not for those tattoos.

She came to him.

"Aren't you coming?"

He shook his head.

"Oh, no," she warned. "You insisted on tagging along and now you have to come in. You can push the cart," she offered as a grand gesture on her part and grabbed his arm, steering him toward the entrance.

He stopped short of the walkway. "I'll wait out here." He nodded to the benches under the overhang, then shoved his hands into his pants pockets.

Calli felt his apprehension. He *really* didn't want to be in the store. How curious. She stepped closer, breaking her no-touching rule and laying a hand on his arm. Muscles tensed beneath her palm as she gazed up into his magnificent eyes. He met her gaze head-on, then looked away, saying nothing. Calli caught the side of his jaw and turned his head until he met her stare again.

"Why don't you want to come in?"

Gabe felt himself being drawn in, like a wave comes naturally to the shore. There was a comfort he'd never known in her eyes, in her hand smoothing rhythmically up and down his arm. And suddenly, he was hungry for it.

His throat worked before he said, "I never had enough cash to ever go in a store this size." He nodded to the huge market, then waited for her disbelief, her pity.

It didn't come.

Calli's heart splintered and she tried to keep tears from forming. What a desolate life he must have led, she thought. And more than he'd believe, she understood.

"But you do now?"

He shrugged. "Never got used to it."

"I know what you mean. Overwhelming, isn't it?"

His brows drew down, suspicion in his eyes.

But Calli kept smoothing his arm, aching to trace the intricacies of his tattoos. "I never had the chance to buy anything for myself, not even a pack of gum, until I was about sixteen."

His chiseled features stretched taut, doubt in his gaze.

"Oh, I'd learned about money, making change, balancing a checkbook, and being polite," she added with a small smile. "But as to actually doing it where anyone could watch—" She shivered dramatically. "I was terrified the first time I had to actually buy clothes. Let alone, ask for help with sizes."

"What did you buy?" he murmured suddenly, huskily.

Her smile was slow, her cheeks staining with color. "Satin panties."

He inched a fraction closer. "What color?" He let his fiery gaze rip and slide over her body.

Calli felt her insides jump to life just then. "Red."

His almost-smile sent her heart tripping up to her throat. "Doesn't surprise me."

She couldn't hide her pleasure in that. That even if everyone else thought she was Suzy Homemaker on the outside, Gabe knew what she hid underneath.

"You don't have to do this with me."

With me, he thought. He couldn't remember when he'd done anything *with* a woman. And never with one like Calli.

"I'm good at this, Gabriel."

He might have rebelled if she hadn't said his name so softly, intimately.

"Make it quick."

She smiled, her hand gliding down to his wrist and pulling him toward the automatic doors. As she grabbed a cart, he pulled away from her touch and Calli tried not to frown at the abrupt gesture. Gabe stayed in the background, off to the side, watchful. Silent. But to her, he looked forlorn and ostracized. Did he think she was embarrassed to be seen with him? She crossed to him, scanning the shelves and selecting products, juggling the items and handing some to him. She inclined her head for him to follow and they dropped them into the cart. He didn't retreat. As she headed for the produce aisle, she noticed how people moved away from him, staring rudely. He seemed oblivious that he was intimidating, almost scary-looking dressed in black and tattooed. Calli touched the flames disappearing beneath his shirtsleeve. He met her gaze, his eyes softer than she'd ever seen them, yet she could feel the tension in him like a coiled wire.

"Are you through?"

She looked down at the nearly empty cart and had to laugh. His stiff posture calmed.

"Ever consider meditation? You need to loosen up."

He stepped closer, his voice low. "You need to hurry up."

He was near enough that she could see every lash surrounding those crystal green eyes, smell the musky scent of him.

"Okay," she said, a little breathless. "Then help shop." She focused on her list. "Flour, sugar, yeast and baking soda."

His eyes widened. "You want me to get it?"

"Can't handle it?" she challenged. He was grinding his teeth, she could tell, and smiled brightly. "Please?"

With a low growl, Gabe moved away. Grinning, Calli watched him as he glared up at the lists posted between each aisle, then marched off. He was intimidated. It was a weakness she never thought to see, yet she was sympathetic. She remembered too clearly how she'd hidden in a dressing room and sobbed because she was so overwhelmed with the wide variety, since she'd worn only uniforms since she was two. Turning back to the vegetables, she selected the best and when she didn't find it, she called for the manager.

Gabe remained back, his arms full, and watched as the manager stepped into the warehouse and came back with another tray of vegetables. He never thought he'd see anyone get so excited over zucchini, but she did. He watched her fingers glide over the long green vegetable and recklessly imagined those hands on his skin. Then he noticed the people staring at him. Gabe glanced to the side and a woman maneuvered her shopping cart well out of his way. A child stood a few feet from him, curiously gazing at his tattoos until his mother yanked him to her side. And when the manager noticed him, he stopped midsentence and stared, too. Calli twisted a look at him and sent him one of her heart-squeezing smiles.

And he was greedy for more of them, more of the way she made him feel when he was near her. Like he *did* matter. He strode forward and dropped the baking supplies into the cart, careful not to smash the vegetables.

She turned toward him slightly. "Now was that so hard?" she said for his ears alone.

Gabe's gaze flashed up, clashing with hers. "No. *Now* are you through?"

She laughed softly. "God, you sound like a kid on a road trip." Then she turned to a mountain of onions and filled a plastic bag.

"Loading up on ammunition?" he growled softly in her ear.

She hefted the onion, her expression sly. "These are white. Only yellow ones for beaning some sense into you." She dropped it into the sack.

"Calli?"

"Hmm?" She was tying off the bag, trying to be nonchalant when her heart was racing around her chest like disturbed bees.

"I was, ah, I mean...I'm—" He looked everywhere but at her.

She blinked, stunned he was tongue-tied. "Are you apologizing?" she whispered.

"I'm trying," he muttered, irritated, then frowned, his gaze searching hers, the unusual brightness of her eyes. Gabe felt something hard shatter inside him. His features tightened. A chill prickled his skin. "Are those *tears?*"

"Of course not." She blinked rapidly. She was touched. Deeply. She knew what that cost him and without thinking of breaking her rules, she stood on tiptoe and brushed her mouth across his. For the briefest moment, he shaped her lips with his.

"Is there anything else I can get you, ma'am?" Calli whirled around, as if just remembering they were in the store.

It took a moment for Gabe to drag his gaze from her, then plant it on the manager, a thought suddenly occurring to him. Calli might be recognizable, because of her job and the high-profile company. Gabe didn't want anyone to know she was in town. It would clue Murdock in if he was still around.

"Peaches and coconuts?"

His expression was apologetic. "Season's over for peaches and we rarely get fresh coconuts."

"Rats," she muttered as they walked away.

"I don't think they carry them," Gabe said lowly.

She laughed, a throaty curl of sound that skated over his skin like a brush of cool wind, before she said, "You know I planned this menu—" she waved the paper "—for the next few days, but didn't ask you what you preferred."

He shrugged. "Anything's fine."

So responsive, she thought with a small smile. "What do you *not* like?"

He stopped and stared off in the distance for a moment. "Grilled cheese, refried beans, tomato soup and macaroni and cheese."

"Yu-uck," she said with feeling. A hint of a smile curved his lips before he looked at her. "I assure you, *those* aren't on the menu."

He peered at it, trying to read her writing. It was in shorthand. Did she do that to her recipes, too?

She headed briskly to the meat counter and purchased all she needed, too aware that he'd moved off to the side and waited, arms folded, his gaze hard and direct on her. She felt hunted instead of guarded. She cast a quick glance at him, noticing the store's customers still made a wide berth to avoid even looking at him. But he didn't seem to care. My Lord, did they think he was going to bite the heads off their children or something? It made her angry to see him treated this way. He'd suffered enough and she inclined her head to him and quickened her pace, selecting spices, oils and pasta.

"You really need all this?" he said from her side.

"I have a new recipe I want to try for Excalibur and what better way to let my creativity flow? I usually have to consult with the guys when I'm in the test kitchen."

"You really don't mind cooking, for us, then?"

He sounded surprised. Did he think cooking was torture?

She grabbed two different grinds of brown sugar off the shelf and glanced at him. "I look at it this way." She dropped them into the cart and pushed on. "I *always* make desserts, and rarely get to prepare anything *normal,* even for myself." She leaned close and whispered, "I have a thing for Chinese takeout, but don't let that get around."

"Your secret's safe," he muttered dryly, staring down at her.

"I knew I could trust you," she said, patting his hand where it lay on the cart handle and trying not to notice how his eyes flared whenever she touched him. "This is my chance to see if I can still create dishes that aren't full of outrageous ingredients nor expensive."

Was she doing that for him and his ranch hands or testing herself? Because she'd proven she was an expert today. But he wasn't going to remind her about lunch. He didn't want to see that smile vanish.

"We're done."

"Thank God," he grumbled as they headed to the checkout where he noticed several men stopping to stare at her as she bent over to unload the groceries onto the conveyor. He moved up behind her, shielding her.

Calli stilled as she placed a sack onto the counter and twisted to look at him. His face was so near she could feel the heat of him, and she let her gaze lower to his chiseled mouth, then back to his eyes. He inhaled through clenched teeth, his leg shifting to brush the side of hers. Heat scrambled up her body to her breasts. Her breath quickened. The noise surrounding them seem to fade.

She didn't think grocery shopping could be so arousing.

But the moment was broken when the cashier called out the total. She found her checkbook, laying it on the counter, but he slapped a hand over it before she could write. She looked at him, straightening. He held her gaze as he withdrew his wallet, pried open the leather and tossed money onto the counter.

Calli slid her checkbook back into her purse, waited till he received his change, then grabbed his hand, lacing her fingers with his. She moved through the narrow aisle and wouldn't let go, shaking her head to the attendant as they passed through the automatic doors. She knew if she broke contact he would retreat into that remoteness she was beginning to sense like a cold wind.

Gabe stared down at the tiny manicured hand clasped in his, delicate against his dark, rough fist. It looked unnatural to him, foreign. He brought his gaze to her profile, to the bright lime-green headband holding back shiny black hair.

Snow White, he thought again as they stopped at the car. He took her keys from her and opened the trunk. With the erotic thoughts going through his head as his gaze shimmered over her body, he sure as hell didn't feel like a Prince Charming.

# Six

"**Y**ou've had a funny look on your face since we left the store," she said as they drove back in the twilight darkness to his place. "What gives?"

He slid her a thin glance, arching a brow, then murmured, "You *don't* want to know."

"Oh, yes I do." That look bordered on decadent.

His fingers flexed on the steering wheel. "Red satin panties."

Calli blushed to the roots of her hair and sank into the seat. "I should never have told you."

And he should never have told her he'd been penniless, he thought, suddenly swamped with those same feelings he had known as a kid. Helpless, vulnerable. Ashamed. Bracing his arm on the door and plowing his fingers through his hair, he wished he could erase the last hour. Well, almost, he admitted, tapping fingers across his smile. Not the way she wasn't embarrassed to be seen with someone as goofy-looking as him, nor her gentle teasing or the way she touched him, breaking her *rules*. And not her tears. That moment was forged in his memory, clear and precise; the way she tilted her head, her glossy blue eyes and quiv-

ering lip. All Gabe wanted to do in that instant was soothe her.
Make her discomfort go away. It wasn't an instinct he was familiar with. No one had ever cried for him. Hell, there were
people who cried because of crud he'd done, but never for giving
a lousy apology. Gabe didn't know what to think about rich and
sophisticated Calli Thornton. Except that she confused the hell
out of him.

He stole a glance at her. Her eyes were closed, her body curled
toward him, her cheek on the back of the seat. Gabe suddenly
felt the weight of the day, too. His body ached and not so much
from hard work, but from fighting his need to lose himself in the
woman dozing beside him. Instinct told him to find the memo,
end his torture, and send her home. And a part of him, which was
growing wider by the day, said keep her here as long as he could
and experience the gentle heart and passion he'd never known
before laying eyes on her.

Great, he was being philosophical now.

His eyes on the road, he cursed softly when he passed the spot
where he'd left his bike and found the Harley gone. He hoped
Bull had taken it back to the ranch. He gunned the engine, thinking about how much work it took to pay for the bike. As he
rounded the long drive and saw the bike against the barn, he
sighed with relief, promising to give Bull a raise when he had the
cash.

Then the old man came rushing from the barn, waving frantically. Gabe pulled under the lights, throwing the car into park.
Calli stirred at the abrupt halt, childishly rubbing her face, then
blinking.

Gabe was out of the car and talking to Bull when she climbed
out.

Gabe looked at her over the top of the car. "The mare's foal-
ing."

"Really?" she squeaked, excited.

"Can you unload the—"

She held up her hand. "Say no more." Immediately, he turned
his back on her and spoke with Bull in hushed, hurried tones.
Calli felt as if a door just slammed in her face. "Can I help?"
she ventured.

"No!" he barked, and she stared, wide-eyed. "No. Just stay away."

Hurt sprang into her eyes and Gabe opened his mouth to say something, then clamped his lips shut and stormed off.

Bull scowled, then shrugged, following his boss.

Calli watched him until he entered the barn, leaving her with ten bags of groceries and confused at the abrupt change. *He's shutting me out, again.* Solemnly, she slid into the driver's seat and started her car, driving it close to the porch and unloading the groceries. After parking her car away from the house, she switched on the outside lights and touched a match to a pair of kerosene lanterns she'd found, hanging them on nails in the support posts.

Knowing Gabe and Bull would be busy most of the night, she prepared a quick snack of hero sandwiches and red corn tortilla chips with dilled chickpea and onion salsa. While she brewed spearmint tea flavored with orange juice, she squinted into the night toward the barn. She couldn't see much, only shadows against the bright lights inside the barn.

*He doesn't want you there,* she thought when she considered going in anyway. It stung that he could close her out so easily. Especially after today. Hefting the tray of food, she brought it into the house, then left a note on the fridge instructing that it was on the dining table. Calli was exhausted. Too much fresh air, she consoled, but knew it was a lie. Too much Gabriel Griffin for one day.

Calli entered her room, kicked off her sandals and fell onto the bed. She was asleep in seconds.

And half an hour later, Gabe stood in the doorway, his lips quirking. She was sprawled facedown across the bed, still dressed and snoring softly. She was too beautiful, he thought, his gaze roaming hotly over her. He'd come in for something to eat and when he found the note and the tray, he'd half expected her to be standing in the middle of the living room, brandishing a frying pan. Bull was in the barn, eating, but Gabe needed to see her without her looking back. Staring into those eyes that mirrored her every emotion, was a little hard to take sometimes.

He shouldn't get comfortable around her, he kept telling himself.

But he kept coming back to the same spot...anywhere near her.

Gently, he pulled a quilt from beneath her feet and covered her. She stirred softly and he lurched back. She jammed a pillow beneath her cheek and wiggled into the mattress. Gabe's gaze moved over her, then her room. Her briefcase lay in the corner. Now would be a good time to search, he thought, but didn't, the strength of his apprehension drawing his gaze repeatedly back to Calli. Before his imagination had her sprawled across his dreams and not that bed, Gabe left.

Calli stirred, blinked, then looked at her watch. Only an hour of sleep? Rolling over, she stretched, noting it was still dark and the faint sound of a vehicle fading into the distance. She left the bed, running her hand through her hair, then a brush. She headed to the bathroom and scrubbed her face, brushed her teeth and was about to step into the bedroom to undress and get into bed when she noticed a sandwich still wrapped and on the tray. She glanced down the hall, wondering if he'd gone to bed without eating or if he was still in the barn. Grabbing an old leather jacket off a coat stand, she donned it against the desert cold, then left the house, noticing Bull's truck was missing. The light from the barn was dimmer and instantly she knew Gabe was still there.

She lit charcoal in the grill and put a pot of coffee on to brew. If he had to stay with the horse all night, he would need something to keep him awake. Any *normal* ranch cook would do the same, she assured herself, impatient for the coffee to perk. She had to hunt, yet found a thermos and a small cooler. She packed the cooler with a few sandwiches and some sliced fruit. Then, grabbing two mugs, she walked toward the barn, the full thermos tucked under her arm. As she approached, her steps slowed and her apprehension grew. He didn't want her here, she reminded herself, then decided that if he wanted her gone, well...she would argue with him.

She stepped into the barn, moving cautiously toward the lit stall. Instantly she lurched back when he leaned out from his position on the floor and pointed a gun at her.

"Hail Mary!" she breathed, and he cursed softly, disappearing from her sight into the stall. She'd never seen him look at her like that. A stare so cold and lifeless it made her shiver. Calli swallowed several times before she ventured closer. At the entrance, she stared down at him. His back was against the wall, knees bent, forearms braced there. He hung his head between his arms. The gun was still in his hand.

"You feel the need for a gun on your own property?"

Slowly he tipped his head back and glared at her. "I have enemies."

"Well, I'm not one of them!" she snapped, still frightened by the vicious look she'd seen in his eyes.

He shrugged. "I thought you were asleep."

"News flash," she said, laughing uneasily. "Now put that thing away."

Gabe twisted to the side, set the safety, and laid the gun in the corner. He returned his gaze to her. She hadn't moved. And he could tell by the way her fingers trembled as she brushed back her hair, he'd scared her. Normally, he would have not given the matter a second thought, considering she'd come unannounced. But this was Calli.

A warm sensation bloomed in his chest when he noticed she was nearly swallowed up in his old leather jacket, the sleeves about five inches too long.

She held out the beat-up cooler and thermos.

"Hungry?"

"You can leave it there." He gestured somewhere behind her. "And go back to the house."

"No."

He arched a brow, his expression threatening. "No?"

"Good. You *can* hear," she said primly, then folded down to the ground adjacent him, uncapping the thermos and pouring some coffee. She held out the mug, smiling.

"Calli." He said it like a warning, taking the cup. In the far corner of the stall, the mare pawed the ground, its body sheened in sweat.

"Yes, Gabriel?"

"I don't need you here."

"Don't need or is it that you don't *want* me here?"

"Both."

That stung. "Too bad, bad boy. You don't own me, we aren't married, not that that would make a difference in decisions about my life, anyway," she told him, pouring coffee for herself. "So, just give it up."

"This is my ranch."

Her gaze flew to his. "Oooh, territorial." She shivered dramatically. "Well, then," she said with an indrawn breath, "I'll be leaving for Mexico in the morning. I guess I'd better pack."

She set the cup aside and stood.

"No!" Then, softer, an irritated growl. "Dammit, you can't."

She peered at him. "And why is that?"

She waited, arms folded, and felt his gaze as it moved up her legs, her torso, to her face. She arched a brow.

Gabe scrambled for a way to keep her from leaving without revealing the truth behind her stay.

"You're broke."

"Only till Monday."

"You're the cook."

That was an even weaker excuse and her sour face said as much. "You could hire anyone from town for this *job*."

"No, I couldn't." There was pause and something flickered in his eyes. "No one would come."

Her shoulders drooped, her mutinous expression fading. "You asked? Placed ads, I mean?"

He nodded. "I seem to scare people off."

The sad fact was that he'd likely alienated himself to the point of being the town mystery, but to not take a job? "Those lousy sons of—"

That she was angry on his behalf stirred an unfamiliar warmth in his chest. "Sit down, Calli." He stared at his lap, hiding a smile. "You're not going anywhere."

"Says you." Fire lit her eyes, her hands on her hips. She wanted an admittance, *something* that would give her a clue to where this man was coming from.

With a speed she couldn't fight, Gabe reached out, grasped the jacket sleeve and yanked. She dropped to the ground, glaring at him. "Yeah, says me. We made a deal. Or are you going to welch out and run for cover?" He arched a brow, the challenge clear.

She looked like an insurgent prepared for battle. "Oh, be serious. You don't scare *me*, Gabriel."

"That a fact?" His gaze slid to her, a wintry stare that chilled her. What did she really know about him? she wondered, staring into his incredible eyes. It didn't matter, she decided in the next heartbeat. The invisible enemies, hotel robbers or guys like Tiny were just insignificant factors. Gabe's insistence that she stay told her he cared, that there was more bark to his lethal bite.

She blinked innocently. "Yes."

His lips quirked. She wasn't backing down and he liked that about her.

The mare suddenly folded to the ground and he moved to the horse, sliding his hands over her distended belly. The beast made a choked sound and Calli knelt.

"Is there anything I can do?"

He shook his head and the animal grunted, hind legs jerking with the waves of pain. "It will be a little longer wait," he said more to himself.

He looked worried, she thought, then opened the cooler and unwrapped a sandwich. When he sat back on his rear, she held it out to him. He accepted it gratefully and though his eyes never left the horse, he devoured the sandwich. Calli ate a half slowly and couldn't take her eyes off him. The slightest movement brought him to the animal. He wiped spit from the horse's mouth, stroked her lovingly and whispered encouragement. His features were hard with purpose, yet his hands gentle as they probed the animal's belly, long brown fingers humming over the dark coat. It was a side of him she never dreamed existed.

Then all hell broke loose. With his mouth full of his last bite, he hovered over the hind end of the beast. "This is it. Go to her head," he said, and didn't wait for a reply. Calli obeyed, shrugging out of his jacket and taking the animal's great head onto her lap.

"Talk to her."

Calli thought that a bit useless, but did it anyway. The horse labored to bring her colt into the world and Calli stroked the damp forelocks, encouraging the mare, but she remained transfixed on the hooves emerging, then a few inches of the regally shaped legs.

She wanted to see more.

Gabe scowled, checked the animal's heartbeat, the growing contraction, then cleared the canal. "Something's wrong," he muttered. Calli looked up, panicked. "The contractions are coming, but—" Gabe bent and probed the mare. "Damn, it's breech!" Immediately he pushed the foal's hooves back inside its mother. For several moments, he manipulated the baby. Blood covered his arms to his elbows.

Gabe sat back on his haunches, dropping his hands. "I can't do this," he muttered. "It won't move."

"Yes, you can," Calli said softly, and his gaze locked with hers. "You have to," she beseeched. "They're depending on you."

Gabe held her gaze trapped in his for a breath longer, then with one hand on the mare's belly, feeling the shape of the colt, he maneuvered the baby into position. The mare whinnied and the contraction forced the hooves out. He grasped them in his big hands. "Come on, girl," he whispered. "Give her to me."

Calli bent low, whispered into the horse's ear, and the animal flinched violently, but it was a long tense moment as the mare strained and strained.

Gabe's gaze flashed to hers. She smiled reassuringly, despite the tears filling her eyes, and they both looked at the mare. The head passed, angled between the legs, then like a boat sliding on the river, the baby slipped completely from its mother. Calli gasped.

Gabe sighed his relief, cleaned the colt's nostrils, pushed it to its mother's side, then finished delivering the placenta. But Calli could do no more than stare at the pair, tears sliding down her cheeks.

"Good girl," Calli whispered, stroking the animal's head. "Look at your baby."

As if the big horse understood, it tipped its head.

Calli laughed, then sniffled, lifting her gaze to Gabe's. "You did it!" she said, awe in her voice.

It gave him a strange feeling deep in his gut. And for the first time in a long while, he simply accepted it.

"I think she—" he gestured to the mare "—would disagree." He stepped back and walked to a standing bucket of water, stripping off his ruined shirt, then sluicing the muck from his arms and chest.

Drying himself, he watched as she laid the mare's head on a pile of straw and came to her knees.

"They would have died without you." She glanced down at mother and son. "I never saw anything like that!" She returned her gaze to his, wiping at her cheeks.

"Thanks, Cal," he whispered softly, sinking to his knees in front of her. He shoved wet hair from his forehead, gazing into her beautiful blue eyes. She seemed keyed-up, ready to explode. It heightened his awareness of her.

Then he smiled.

All crinkling eyes, dimples and straight white teeth. A full-blown, happy-to-be-alive smile.

It knocked her breathless.

"No, thank you!" she shrieked as she launched into him, her arms looping around his neck. They tumbled to the floor outside the birthing stall, Calli sprawled across him. "Oh, Gabe, that was the most incredible experience!" Her words heated the side of his throat.

He chuckled deeply. "Glad you could enjoy it." He stared at the ceiling, feeling her body's push and give against his own. Slowly his arms came around her. "You're breaking your own rules," he murmured, his hands on her trim waist.

"I know," she said into the crook of his neck, and Gabe realized she was sobbing. He held her back, ducking his head to look her in the eye.

"Cal?"

She sniffled. Then she tipped her head and met his gaze. Gabe's expression crumbled.

"Don't cry. Please don't."

"I can't help it." Her lower lip trembled pitifully.

"Ah, jeez," he groaned, then urged her head to his shoulder. Her arms tightened around his neck, clinging.

"I feel so foolish."

"It's okay," he murmured, pressing his lips to her temple. Gradually she quieted, her tense body deflating against his. Gabe was anything but relaxed. He rolled to the side, tucking her close to his chest, and closed his eyes. It felt wonderful just to hold her. They stayed like that for several moments before she lifted her head and met his gaze.

"Break another rule with me," she said, and cupped the back of his head, drawing him down to meet her mouth. At the first touch, Gabe devoured her like his last meal, his lips and tongue rolling hotly over her mouth. She moaned deep in her throat, arching closer to his long frame as passion ignited and burned. She let herself be swept along, let him take control, savoring him, the weight of his hands scraping down her back, her hips, to her buttocks. He cupped her, pressing her deeply into him, to his hardness, and Calli gasped against his mouth. But he didn't stop kissing her and hovered over her body, his mouth blistering wildly over hers.

There was freedom in touching Calli, he thought, a feeling he wanted to grasp and hold tight. Caution faded, passion raged and Gabe stole all he could in the dimness of the barn. He never wanted anything more than he wanted Calli.

And she gave, willingly, urging his weight onto hers, her hands caressing his warm bare chest. She felt every indentation, every ripple of muscle, and he groaned into her mouth, lushly licking the outline of her lips, then driving his tongue deeply between. *More,* he thought. *I need more.*

Calli could feel his hand slide along her thigh, his fingers curl behind her knee, drawing it up. The motion spread her, fit her tightly, intimately, to the heat of him, the contours of his hard body molding to hers like a second skin, the softness of her yielding to the shape of his arousal. He rocked against her and her breath staggered in her throat, her body answering him. Then he enfolded her breast, his thumb brushing ever-deepening circles around her nipple hidden beneath the cloth. His mouth softened on hers, coaxing her desire to rage with his, and then his hand was beneath her shirt, inside her bra and she swore she didn't breathe until his fingers touched bare skin. She whimpered against his mouth, eager to have him naked against her and when he pushed up her shirt, exposing her, she held her breath in anticipation of his mouth on her skin.

It didn't happen and she opened her eyes. He was breathing as heavy as she, frowning. Not at her, but the horse.

The colt neighed sluggishly. Gabe was off her and at the baby's side in a heartbeat. Calli struggled upright, righting her clothing, a flush of embarrassment and unspent desire coloring her skin. Gabe pulled the colt gently away from its mother and put on a stethoscope and listened for a heartbeat. He nodded to himself, then, letting the scope hang from his neck, he dragged blankets from a pile to cover the baby. Then he stood, grabbed the bucket and vanished out the stall. She inched toward the foal, stuffing hay to cushion its head. Gabe returned with a full bucket of water, pausing briefly in the doorway. She let her gaze climb up his body to his face, the stark outline of his arousal evident against his snug jeans. When she met his gaze his lips quirked, a little cynically, and her heart sank to her stomach. That coldness reminded her how easily Gabe could turn to Angel.

He cleaned the colt, then dried him like a father would his child, his darkly tanned muscles jumping and flexing. He covered the baby warmly, then braced his back against the wall and drew the gangly colt's head onto his lap. He held it, one hand on its chest, the other stroking its proud head. After a moment, he lifted his gaze.

Gabe's expression tightened. She was kneeling back on her calves, her hands clasped on her lap. There was straw in her hair and her lips were swollen and bruised. She looked a little lost.

Calli didn't deserve to be laid down in a barn. She deserved a bed and silk sheets and room service. And someone other than him.

Then she turned to the mugs, knocked over in their tussle in the hay. Gabe cringed at the thought of what she must feel like, summarily dismissed because of the colt. Yet she poured more coffee and handed him the steaming mug. He accepted it, but didn't sip. It amazed him, that flash-fire hunger they shared. His body still burned with the effects of her, of holding her in his arms, feeling her hands on his skin. His jeans tightened across his hips. His suffering was well deserved. He should never have let it get that far.

She shifted, Indian style, and nodded to the colt before she said, "Is he going to be all right?"

"Yeah, just had a tough time getting here."

"Should we contact a vet or the owner?" She was aware that he only boarded and trained horses.

"I am the owner."

She blinked, noticing the pride in his voice.

"It was a deal I made with the mare's owner." A pause and then, "I can't afford a vet."

She nodded and didn't bother to offer to pay for the vet call. She knew he would refuse unless it meant the colt's life. "What are you going to call him?"

Gabe looked down at the newborn foal. "Horse."

"Oh, for heaven's sake! That's not a name, it's a noun!"

He scowled at her.

"He needs a majestic name, Gabe." His scowl deepened. "I mean, look at him." The colt was solid black with a creamy beige splotch at his forehead. "He looks like dark bittersweet chocolate."

Gabe took a peek under the blanket. "He's a she, Cal."

Calli blushed. "Oh."

"Since you don't like my choices, maybe you should choose a name."

She blinked. "Me?" She shook her head.

He shrugged. "Then it's Horse."

"Okay, okay." She put up her hand. "Let me think." She focused on her coffee mug, her hands around it to keep warm. Gabe reached out and snatched up his jacket, tossing it to her. She slipped it on, murmuring her thanks, her lovely face still marked with concentration.

"Eclair."

"No."

Her gaze flashed up and collided with his. A tiny smile worked over her lips.

"Divinity?"

He shook his head.

"Killer Death?"

His brows rose into his forehead.

She shrugged, chagrined. "It's a fudge cake."

"I'm sure you'll think of something," he said tiredly, and Calli realized what a full day he'd put in. At least she'd had a chance to catch a bit of sleep.

"It has to be a good one, Gabriel." Gabe closed his eyes, loving every time she said his name.

Rummaging in the cooler, she took out half a sandwich and offered it to him. He shook his head and she shrugged, biting into it. It was gone in minutes, yet Gabe simply watched her. She leaned close to stroke the colt, then turned her concern to the mother, taking a rag and wiping the tired animal's big head. She looked so tiny against the animal and even as she offered the horse a drink from a tin cup, he recognized the mothering nature in her, in her assuring whispers, the tender touches. It was hard to believe the same woman was untamed and savage in his arms a few moments ago. For a fleeting moment Gabe imagined her with children, her body full with life, and his lips curved into a tender smile. Then it vanished.

Dreams are for people with cash and an education, he thought cynically.

She repacked the cooler and closed the thermos, then settled down beside him against the stall.

"You can go back to the house," he said, yet inside, his mind was screaming at him to shut up and take what he could get of her company. This war inside him was going to kill him.

"No, thank you," she replied with a hint of defiance, and snuggled into the jacket, staring at the animals. "Where did you learn so much about horses?"

Gabe hesitated and she tilted a look at him.

"Well?"

Gabe plucked a piece of straw from the colt's face, rubbing it between his fingers. How he got here wasn't something he wanted to tell her and he considered glossing over the truth. Then he decided that the best way to get her to back off was to give it to her quick and hard. "I got caught burglarizing this guy's house."

Her eyes widened. "You were a thief?"

"A cat burglar."

She made a sour face. "Apparently not a very good one."

His glare was thin and piercing, but Calli simply stared back and smiled benignly, waiting.

"Do go on," she cooed.

He sighed irritatedly and the words were practically ripped from him. "He didn't press charges or call the cops."

"Sounds stupid."

He arched a brow in her direction.

"You committed a crime and were caught." She shrugged leather-clad shoulders. "By all rights you should have gone to jail."

"Well, I didn't," he snapped. "But that doesn't mean I haven't."

She twisted toward him, bracing her shoulder on the wall. "I'm not impressed, Gabriel, nor am I quivering with fear just because you've served time. What I do want to know is what happened to your victim?"

Gabe considered telling her to stuff her curiosity in her pocket and take herself back into the house, but her patient tone told him she wasn't going anywhere till she got her answers. "He made a call, gave me a name and address, and told me if I didn't want to go to prison, to show up at the appointed time."

"And that was at a ranch?"

Gabe nodded, thinking about the backbreaking work he did for next-to-nothing for pay. Yet the satisfaction of doing it by the law, for the first time in years, was what had kept him there.

"So why do you think this compassionate citizen gave you a break?"

"Hell, I don't know!" But he did. Daniel came to see him after he'd been at the ranch for a few months. He'd checked on him without Gabe knowing and told him that if he'd skipped, he would have called the cops. And one night over a beer, Daniel admitted to being in the same situation as Gabe, years before. Penniless, homeless, and without an education to get him a decent job.

"How old were you?"

He slid her a quick glance. "When I started being a thief or when I stopped?"

"Stopped."

"About twenty, I guess."

"Now I'm impressed."

He scowled. "At what?"

"You stuck it out. You accepted this man's challenge. You could have kept going, Gabriel. You were free. But you chose not to run." She looked down at the colt sleeping on his lap and ran her fingers over its beautiful face. "And now look where you are. What you have to show for your hard work."

"What I have is a run-down ranch, very little cash, debt up to my eyeballs and one colt I can call my own!"

She lifted her gaze, unaffected by his quick temper. "But you had nothing before. Nothing."

He stared into her soft blue eyes and saw hope and confidence. His throat worked. "Damn, Calli."

She smiled tenderly, reaching out to brush back a lock of dark hair from his forehead. "Run-down, debts and all, it's still *yours,* Gabriel. Be thankful. It's more than I have."

He scoffed, aware she had a car that was worth more than his entire ranch.

"I have clothes, some housewares and a car that the bank will own till I'm forty. My apartment's rented. Oh, I have a little nest egg stashed away, very little, but I never took the risk of sinking it into, say, a restaurant or a bakery shop. Not like you. I never had the guts."

"But I was a thief." Didn't she hear him?

"Was," she reminded, then wiggled next to him, yawning hugely. "Big deal. I burned Sister Mary Margaret's habit. What could be worse than leaving a nun naked?" She closed her eyes. Then she was sinking against his shoulder, asleep.

Gabe looked down at her, her face serene, her lips parted. He stroked black hair from her face and bent to brush his lips against hers. Her mouth responded naturally for the briefest moment, then she sighed into her dreams. Gabe swept his arm around her and she settled into the crook of his shoulder. He tipped his head back against the hardwood wall and for the first time in years, found a little peace.

# Seven

Calli woke to find herself alone, neither the mare nor the colt in the stall. Or Gabriel. Stretching, she tossed off the horse blanket and sat up, scrubbing her face with her hands, then rising. She wrapped the leather jacket tightly against the morning chill. Lord, who ever said the desert was always hot? she wondered as she headed out of the barn. She stopped short at the sight of the mare and her baby in the corral, the colt moving on wobbly legs. Then her gaze shifted to the man with one foot on the lower fence rail, his forearms braced on the top. He'd showered and changed already and she glanced at her watch and wondered if he'd ever slept. It was only a little after six.

"Good morning," she murmured, and he tilted his head to look at her. Though he was wearing sunglasses, she felt his gaze move over her from head to foot and back.

"Morning," came curtly.

Calli ignored it. He's just overtired, she thought. "I can't believe they're walking." She climbed onto the top rail, sitting close to him.

"The mare was up a half hour after the birth. The colt about an hour later," he felt obligated to say as he looped a lead rope around his hand. How could she smell so good after sleeping in a barn all night?

"Amazing," she whispered, watching the colt take several shaky steps, then looked up at him. "Personally I would be sleeping the day away after delivering a hundred pounds of horseflesh. Females—" She shrugged. "Go figure."

Gabe's lips twitched with a smile, then just as quickly, it vanished.

He looked weary, she thought. "Did you ever get any sleep?" Concern laced her voice.

"Enough," he said, and from behind the dark glasses, Gabe let his gaze slide over her face, the smudged mascara from her tears, the bits of hay in her hair. Yeah, he'd slept all right. After fighting the press of her body against his, he'd given in and held her warmly against him until dawn. It was the calmest night he'd had in years. And sunrise reminded him that it wouldn't last. Damn. Even if he wanted to think in the future tense, he wouldn't. He had nothing to offer her except his name on a mortgage, anyway. Least now she knew it. But he resented that she could pry his past from him so easily and he was ticked at himself for getting hopeful and telling her, just to see what she'd do. Her quick dismissal of his failings and her admiration over his victories touched him in places he thought were dried up or dead. It wasn't the reaction he'd anticipated. And it made him feel vulnerable. *She* made him vulnerable. Wanting her, touching her...needing her, was a weakness he couldn't afford or deserve. Not even with the wild desire constantly flaming between them. Gabe knew the reality. He was a fascination, a little taste of danger maybe, to a woman who'd been sheltered.

And when she found out she was his assignment, that he'd followed her before they'd met, baited her into coming here so he could watch over her and still keep his ranch afloat? And when he had to search her things for the private memo? Then what?

It would destroy her.

Lord, he should never have told her anything about himself. He didn't want her to like him, to be accepting or so damn open and forgiving. It would make it easier to live with himself, he thought, if she hated him now instead of later. This strange relationship had already gone too far, too quickly.

Her brows drew down. "What's the matter?" She'd felt the change in him the instant she'd walked up, like a heaviness settling around him, but now it was worse.

"Nothing. There will be two more for breakfast," he said as if informing the hired help of changes. He made to duck beneath the rail.

"Well, something is. Talk to me, Gabriel."

Straightening, he steeled himself against the sound of her voice and spared her a hard glance. "Back off, Calli."

She blinked, hurt springing through her. "What the heck is that supposed to mean?"

Gabe almost crumbled. The stricken look on her face was enough to bring down a mountain. But he didn't trust it. "It means mind your own business, *city girl*. I'm not your charity case to be saved. I have work to do and so do you." He ducked under the rail and walked to the mare, clipping a lead to her bridle.

Calli's lip quivered and she bit down on it. She wished she had an onion. No, she corrected, a bushelful. *City girl*. He was reminding her that she wasn't a part of his world, no matter what she did.

"What happened between last night and this morning?" she shouted. No answer. "Can't you just talk with me? What's so hard about that?" When he clucked his tongue and the mare walked after him, Calli hopped off the rail. She took two steps toward the house, then looked back. "You're scared, Gabriel Griffin." His head jerked up and she met his wintry gaze head-on. "Of me. And that wall you conveniently build isn't keeping me out, it's keeping *you* in."

His smirking look said that was fine with him.

"Fine. I hope the isolation offers pleasant company." For the next fifty years.

She left and didn't see him watch her storm into the house. Slamming the door, she strode into her room, stripping out of her clothes, slapping them over the back of a chair before donning her robe. She grabbed her cosmetic bag and headed for the shower, her hands trembling. She rinsed and washed and scrubbed her hair so hard her scalp stung. Standing under the spray, she shaved her legs and nicked her knee, the soap burning into the open cut. She hissed and fanned it, hopping on one foot, then fell back against the wall, letting it sting, letting it bleed. She gripped the chain and water cascaded over her, hiding her tears. He'd done that intentionally, returned her to the out-of-place misfit she'd felt like all her life. Insignificant and meaningless. Unworthy. The man didn't know what he had, she thought. More than her, more than most. He had a place to belong, to grow roots if he wanted.

She didn't belong anywhere. Again. And Gabriel just made it clear that she didn't belong anywhere near him.

A few minutes later, Gabe was in the barn clearing away the soiled hay, replacing it with fresh, when Bull filled the entrance.

"See you managed well enough." Bull inclined his head toward the paddock beyond the walls.

Gabe glanced up, noticed his shirt said Life Is Short, Eat Dessert First and wondered if he'd bought it just for Calli. Her hurt face flashed in his mind and his lips pulled into a grim line. He went back to forking hay. "Breech birth. Was tough for a few minutes."

Bull nodded, understanding. "See Miss Calli took good care of you." He nudged the cooler and thermos still laying by the doorway.

Gabe didn't respond; Bull's curiosity was like a terrier with a bone.

"You didn't do nothing you ain't 'posed to, did you, son?"

Gabe's head jerked up, his eyes narrowing. "What the hell do you mean by that?"

Bull took a step back, putting up both hands. "Nothing, nothin'…just that she's beatin' the heck out of bread dough, slamming pot and pans and looks dang mad."

Gabe ground his teeth and pitched hay. "She'll get over it."

"Yeah, sure she will," Bull muttered, turning his back on him.

Gabe threw down the pitchfork and stomped outside, pulling his sunglasses from where they were hooked at the neck of his shirt and putting them on. She was like a tornado without direction, moving from table to counter to grill. And Bull was right. It was obvious to anyone that she was steaming. He started to cross to the kitchen, then thought better of it. He made the mess, now he had to deal with it. It *had* to be this way. *Did it?* a voice in the recesses of his tired brain pestered.

A white van pulled into the drive, two familiar teenagers slowly climbing out. Gabe forced himself to turn away from her and give the boys their instructions.

Calli hadn't looked in Gabe's direction when the two teenage boys showed up. Nor when he introduced his part-time ranch hands, though the teenagers looked rougher than gravel. As Gabe set them to work, she couldn't help notice the similarities between him and the boys. Though they didn't sport near as many tattoos, the dark clothes and constant glaring at each other rang familiar. *Tales From the Hood,* she thought with a quick glance to where Gabe had them hauling hay bales. Gabe had made them get rid of the plaid shirts and she'd heard him say this was his "turf" and they followed his rules.

Geyser and Deek. Certainly interesting names, she mulled, trying to keep her hurt back and her temper forward. She set the table beneath the long wide porch, venting her frustration on slapping the flatware onto the table. She kept telling herself she was a professional and should rise above this, but she was too hurt to make the climb.

Gabe cringed when she beat a metal spoon and pot together, calling them to the table. The boys dropped their baling hooks and started for the house, but Gabe called them back, making them wash up and don their shirts. But when the boys and Bull headed toward the table, Gabe couldn't take his eyes off the woman standing at the far end of the porch, chopping vegetables with a huge cleaver.

He stopped short of the shade and stared at her. She kept her attention focused on the peppers she was mincing. He turned his gaze to the table and his eyes widened. There were pancakes with strawberries, Spanish omelets, hash browns, Canadian bacon, sausage, biscuits with boysenberry jam, along with fresh coffee and orange/pineapple juice to wash it all down. As if any of them could eat all this.

"Good God, Calli."

"Yes," she sang sweetly. "Is there a problem?" Though her voice was angelic, she held the knife in her hand like a tomahawk.

Gabe lashed a hand at the table. "Who do you expect to eat all this?"

She sent him a brittle smile that didn't meet her eyes and turned her gaze to the teenagers, gesturing with the knife. "Growing boys eat a lot."

Geyser and Deek glared up at her from their plates. Oops, she thought. Guess they don't think of themselves as boys.

Calli glanced uncertainly at Bull, avoiding looking at Gabe altogether. Bull smiled reassuringly and filled his plate. The boys ate as if they hadn't in a week. Gabe simply stared at her, scowling.

Calli moved to the far end of the kitchen area to the long worktable. She measured and sifted flour into a large silver mixing bowl, dissolved yeast into another, stirred in buttermilk, then kneaded the bread dough.

"Whatcha making, Miss Calli?" Bull called.

She looked to where he sat a few yards away under the shade of the porch and shrugged. "Not sure yet, maybe a currant bread or a jalapeño loaf." She cleaned off her hands and strode to the *horno,* stoking the fire high.

"How can you do that? I mean, start mixin' stuff together when you don't know whatcha want in the end?"

She shoved in another log, then slid her gaze to Gabe's, then Bull's. "Most breads are very basic recipes, Bull. All it takes is a few extra ingredients to make the difference. Sometimes I never know what I'll get in the end." Briefly she caught Gabe's gaze. "That's the risk. I like it."

Gabe's eyes narrowed on her, then he slanted a look at Bull. Bull grunted, then focused on his breakfast. Gabe kept his gaze on her.

But Calli couldn't take it, not the emptiness and abandonment she felt. It was too much like when she was a kid—thrown away. She turned back to the dough, kneading it with a vengeance before dropping the lump into an oiled bowl. She tossed a dish towel over it, then cleaned up her mess. She banged pot and pans, nearly broke a dish and cut her finger on a knife she'd forgotten was in the dishwater. She stilled, wrapping her hand in towel and holding pressure. This isn't working, she thought, bowing her head and praying she wouldn't cry.

"Calli?" Gabe knew she'd hurt herself; he'd heard the soft hiss of pain.

Yet she kept her back to them and in a soft voice said, "When you're finished, just set the dirty dishes on the counter, please." Then she marched into the house without a backward glance.

Gabe slumped in his seat and shoved his plate back. Geyser and Deek exchanged a glance, then snickered. Gabe leaned across the table, in their faces until both boys ducked their heads. Bull gave him a what-the-hell's-goin'-on look. Gabe ignored it, grabbed a biscuit from the platter and tore into it, still staring at the spot where she'd disappeared.

This is what you wanted, he told himself. You wanted her to hate you and now she does. But as the others cleared away their dishes and left him alone, Gabe had a strong feeling he'd just trashed the best thing to happen along for him—since Daniel had caught him lifting his wife's heirloom jewelry.

Gabe was dead tired by the time the van came to pick up the teenagers to take them back to juvenile hall. The image of Calli's hurt, the words she'd said to him in the paddock this morning, kept playing over and over in his head. He'd tried not to think about her, but the beautiful sound of her laughter, laughter she shared with the others, kept taunting him. He could hardly look at her without feeling her pain.

As the boys crossed to the vehicle, Gabe watched as she left the porch and called out to them, running to catch up, and pressing a fat brown sack into each of their hands. The teens stared at it, Deek bringing it to his nose and inhaling whatever she'd prepared for them. Desserts, Gabe thought, since she'd asked them their favorites. It was the first time he'd seen either Deek or Geyser smile. She waved as the van pulled away, then spun around and walked back to the porch. The scent of grilled beef had filled the air for the past hour and now, he was starving. But having dinner with her was going to be torture, he thought grimly. It was damn hard work avoiding those wounded blue eyes. He washed up and called to Bull as he headed toward the set table.

"Can't," Bull hollered as he walked to his truck. "Got a hot date."

Gabe swung around. "A date?"

"It's Saturday night, son." He wiggled his brows, then slid behind the steering wheel.

Gabe stood in the center of the dirt drive and watched the red truck bounce down the road before facing the house. The kitchen was empty, the cookware cleaned, counters cleared, and no Calli.

He moved closer and under the light of the kerosene lamps she'd grown fond of was a place setting laid out for him. Platters and bowls were covered with cloths. He turned one back and his mouth watered at the aroma of barbecued beef. Yet it was apparent that she wasn't going to join him. Gabe told himself he didn't care, that he didn't need anyone, and he pulled out the chair. He sat, filling his plate. For long moments, he stared down at the meal, his tired body craving the fuel. Then he lifted his gaze and looked out over his land, the empty paddock, the single light hanging over the barn entrance, the driveway where her car and his truck and bike were separated by nearly fifty yards. Like us. In the distance, a coyote howled, and alone, under the yellow glow of light, Gabe picked up his fork and took a bite. He ate, feeling the weight of his actions. He was wrong. It wasn't easy to live with her hating him. It wasn't even living.

Calli heard the door rattle and didn't look up from the book she was reading. Not that she knew what it was about. She'd seen him out there, alone, finishing his dinner. He'd looked so lonely she'd almost gone to him.

Almost. That's what he wanted, she thought again. And she hoped he enjoyed it, because she didn't.

She flinched when he suddenly appeared in the doorway. He stared; she could feel the weight of his gaze without looking. It wasn't fair that she felt so much around this man.

"What are you reading?"

She closed her eyes briefly against the sound of his voice, the rough, deep texture stealing over her skin. She didn't want to be near him right now, afraid she'd throw herself at him or something equally as ridiculous. For a few desperate seconds she battled between staying and having it out with him—or a quick cut-and-run. Self-preservation won and she left the sofa, handing over the book without looking at him before she headed to her room.

Gabe stood in his living room and watched her leave, watched the subtle shift of her satiny robe against her skin, the body lightly clad beneath. Then he heard the soft click of the door. And his imagination exploded with the image of her slipping out of the robe and sliding beneath the bedsheets. His arms suddenly ached with their emptiness. He wished things were different, wished he was worthy of a woman like her, wished he had met her under different circumstances. He wished he didn't want what she had so bad he couldn't think straight anymore.

*That wall you conveniently build isn't keeping me out, it's keeping* you *in.*

Don't you see? he thought dispiritedly. That's where *I* belong.

He dropped her book and crossed to the hall, pausing at her bedroom door. For a fraction of a second, he raised his hand to knock, then clenched his fist against following through. He lowered his arm and stared at the beam of light coming from beneath the door, imagining her bathed in candlelight. He had no right to be here. No right! He spun away and headed to the shower, hoping the cold water would deflate his desire—and his need to feel anything besides this aching.

He gave up trying to sleep around sunrise, and he blamed Calli, then blamed himself. Throwing his legs over the side of the bed, Gabe pulled on a pair of jeans and raked his hand through his hair. He needed coffee and paused in the bathroom to brush his teeth and splash water on his face. He wasn't looking forward to another day like yesterday, he thought, leaving the bathroom to make a pot of coffee. As he passed her room, he heard a sound, a whimper, and his heart dropped to his feet. He rapped on the door.

"Calli?"

"What!"

Okay, he thought, she had a right to be ticked at him. "You all right?"

"Fine!"

Another grunt, a whimper.

"What the hell is going on in there?"

"Not that it's any of your business, but there are two devastatingly gorgeous men in here arguing over who gets to make love to me."

Gabe smirked. "Yeah, right."

"I told them they both could." A pause, then, "Rats!"

Gabe opened the door and swallowed his breath. She was on the bed, one leg Indian style, the other stretched up alongside her head. When she realized he was there, she dropped her leg and threw her robe over her bare skin.

"Is there a problem?"

"Nothing that I can't handle." The flush of embarrassment fled through her face. His gaze dropped to the manicure kit spread out on the bed. "A splinter," she said when he scowled, and wished he'd leave.

"Want some help?"

"No!" she snapped. Then softer, "No, thank you. I can manage just fine."

"Did you get it out?"

She shook her head.

"Then you aren't managing *just fine.*"

"Well, I certainly don't need your help!"

Gabe felt her hurt like a fresh, hard slap. "Look, Calli. I know you're ticked off—"

"Ha!" she snapped. "You don't know *anything.*"

He took a step closer and she pulled her legs in protectively, then winced.

He stood by the bed, gazing down at her. It was clear she'd been up for a little while. Her hair was brushed and she smelled like wildflowers. He sat on the bed and she immediately scooted back.

"Where's the splinter?"

"It's fine really, go away. Please." She shooed him, then pushed the creamy satin robe tighter around her throat.

Gabe tried not to notice the lush shape of her body against the fabric, the hint of scalloped lace edging her bra.

"Gonna kill you to ask me for help, isn't it?"

"I don't want it, Gabe."

"But you need it."

She said nothing, her lips pressed tight.

He sighed and wrestled the tweezers from her clenched fist. She stared mutinously back. "Too proud?" he goaded. He loved the way her eyes flared with her temper.

"Look who's talking," she scoffed under her breath. But she did need his help. It was a humiliating fact and she decided that she *could* be objective. "Okay, fine, you take it out. But don't say I didn't warn you."

He frowned. She leaned back against the headboard, against the mound of pillows, her foot sliding luxuriously against his thigh as she unfolded her leg. His frown deepened and slowly she pulled back the robe, liking that his Adam's apple bobbed in his throat, enjoying the way his gaze kept bouncing from her eyes to her bare leg.

Gabe felt his body tense with each inch of skin she revealed, the slow drag of fabric taunting him.

"It's there," she said, pointing to her inner thigh. "Must have gotten it when I was sitting on the railing."

His gaze flew to hers. Eyes locked and Gabe remembered her hurt, the utter loneliness he'd felt yesterday without her teasing, her bright smiles. It felt as if it had been a week instead of a few hours since he'd looked into those expressive blue eyes.

Then she arched a brow, cynical and bitter, and Gabe knew again the damage he'd done. He focused on the red skin surrounding the splinter and told himself he could do this without getting carried away. He leaned over, but the lack of light made it hard to see. He reached out and pulled the oil lamp closer, and in the back of his mind, he wished he'd had electricity run into the house. He tried again and she winced, inhaling sharply.

"I can't see it well enough to get it." Without thought, he shifted her so her legs dangled off the bed, then he slid to the floor, between her knees, bracing his arm and torso on the mattress before drawing her calf across his bent knee. He peered, catching her skin between thumb and forefinger and plucking at the sliver of wood. She hissed and tensed and he glanced up. She was propped on her elbows, a bland look on her face. Then his gaze slid down to where the robe parted, exposing the cream lace panties shielding the darkness of her. He ground his teeth and tried again for the splinter. In seconds, he held it up for her approval, then tossed the tweezers onto the bed, immediately reaching for the bottle of antiseptic and balls of cotton.

"I can do that." She tried to take it.

He pushed her hand away and blotted the wound. A tiny shriek worked in her throat, her muscles flexing, and Gabe instinctively blew on the area.

"Better?"

She nodded shakily. "Thank you."

If Gabe was aware of his position before, now it was intensified. He let his gaze linger, hunger over her as he smoothed his hand up her bare leg.

She scooted back. "What are you doing?"

He shrugged. "Checking for more splinters."

His little half-smile made her weak for more. "There aren't any."

But he couldn't resist the temptation of her skin and pressed his mouth against her inner thigh. Calli stiffened, her body betraying her. An instant later, his tongue slicked over the same spot, climbing higher, closer to the heat of her. His breath bathed her, sinking into her body as if he'd sunk a finger inside. A soft sound worked in her throat, and for a heartbeat she closed her eyes and absorbed. Then suddenly she scrambled back, curling her legs in and covering herself.

"No." She kept shaking her head as if she was trying to convince herself. "I'm not falling for this again, Gabe," she said with a steely look at him. "I'm not your toy and..."

"And what?" he said, standing.

She lurched off the bed, belting her robe tightly. "*And* nothing is going to happen here!"

"What did you think was going to happen?"

She scoffed, tossing her hair back with a shake of her head. "How about you kissing me and touching me, then—" her voice fractured "—you *hurting* me." She turned her back on him, bracing her palms on the dresser.

"Calli, I—"

"What, Gabriel? What will you say to me this time? That you're sorry. No. I don't think so. That you didn't meant it? Oh, I *know* you did. You've made it painfully clear that the door is locked and no one has the key." He took a step closer and she straightened, staring at his reflection in the mirror. Her eyes rapidly filled with tears. "My lord, you make it so hard to be your friend."

"You make it too easy."

She licked her lips. "Is that so bad?"

He looked at the floor, his thumbs hooked in his pants pockets. "I haven't had many."

He doesn't trust her friendship, she realized. He doesn't see why anyone would want to be his friend. She'd seen how people in the grocery store treated him. He was probably waiting for her to act the same way. Deliberately, she tried for patience. "I told you when I came here that I didn't expect anything from you. Well, now I do."

He met her gaze in the mirror, a shock of dark hair spilling over one eye. He was devastating to look at, she thought, taut brown muscles, the dangerous signature of artwork on his arms, the gold earring. He took her breath away every time she met his pale green gaze.

"I'm asking you to forget what you *think* I want and just...*be Gabriel*. I don't need to know the gory details of your past if you don't want to offer them. They don't matter right now, this minute."

"They will."

"Stop looking for trouble!" she raged. "And before you get all macho on me—" She put up a hand. "I *don't* want to know how many women you've had in this room."

"None."

"Well, then, in that bed."

"Never." He advanced slowly and awareness sank through her body.

"Oh, hell, on this dresser," she practically yelled.

He stopped directly behind her, his breath, his words, brushing her neck. "Just you."

She stared defiantly at his reflection. "You tried that and failed."

"Did I?" he growled, and his reasons for pushing her away faded to the fierce longing to touch her, smell her…feel her.

He was up against her, his front to her back and Calli couldn't move as his breath fanned her ear, his words so rough with urgency she barely heard them.

"I need to hold you, Calli."

It sounded like a desperate plea dragged from the darkness. Then without waiting for her response, his arms slowly wrapped around her, one across her breasts and gripping her shoulder, the other around her waist, his big hand splayed across her hip. The sight in the mirror was startling, his arms, dark and tattooed against the pristine sheen of her cream satin robe, her skin. He simply held her, as if waiting for her to shove him away, patient, timeless.

*This is Gabriel,* she thought. She was aware of him, every nuance, the shadow of his beard against her hair, his bare chest, sleek and hairless, his snug jeans, the top button carelessly left undone, the strength of his thighs laying along the length of hers. And the heat between them. He was like a sleek panther on the prowl, scenting her, content, yet tense, prepared to spring. Calli erupted with sensation, her mind and body vividly alive by the mere thought of his need to touch her. Then his dark head lowered, his lips pressing to her throat. She sighed softly, yet couldn't take her gaze off their reflection. She covered his forearm with her palm, then reached up and dove her fingers into his hair. He groaned and deepened the warm press of his mouth on her throat. So gentle.

She whispered his name and Gabe tipped his head and stared. This was them, he thought. Light and dark, unblemished and the tarnished. He offered danger and uncertainty. She offered forgiveness. And hope. He'd known that so rarely in his life that he wanted it desperately, needed the seduction of Calli. In her own odd little way, she kept the cold somewhere off in the distance. She was suddenly the only spark left to him. A tiny voice in him goaded that he might never get another chance with a woman like this, that even if he wasn't in her league, even if he couldn't understand why she felt about him the way she did, he could accept it, for a little while. Like a gift from a forgetful god. Forget what would happen in a few days. Forget that he might mangle everything because this was unfamiliar. He wanted her with him at any cost. Because with Calli, he felt clean and deserving. My God, he felt redemption in simply touching her.

"Gabriel," she whispered into his thoughts. "I have to go."

He met her gaze in the mirror, his narrowing sharply. "Where?"

"To mass."

His scowl deepened.

She sifted her fingers through his hair, loving that he simply held her. "You know, church? It's Sunday."

It hit him all over again what kind of woman he held in his arms. "Then maybe," he said tipping her head, "you should have something to confess." His tongue outlined the curve of her lips, a slow lush motion as his hand slid down her stomach and covered her softness.

"Oh, Gabriel." She shuddered helplessly and he kissed her again and again. With infinite care, he loosened her sash. Calli caught his hand. "No." The protest sounded mild, even to her.

"Is this what you want? Tell me," he whispered, parting her robe. The cool morning air caressed her skin and he waited, breathing in her scent, giving her a chance to deny him. She didn't. "You're so beautiful," he murmured, and watched his hand slide over her breasts covered in cream lace.

Calli moaned deliciously and closed her eyes.

"No," came the sultry command. "Watch us."

And she did. His broad hands caressed her stomach, slid languorously over her hips to her thighs. His fingers dipped between. And she pressed back against him. Then his touch rose again, the heat of it searing her skin as his fingertips came together and slid downward beneath the edge of her panties. Her breath caught and

he touched the downy softness. Calli thought she'd come apart
right there. The woman reared by nuns told herself to end this
before she surrendered and yet another woman, the one who
stepped into a bar seeking risk, said, *Here it is, take.*

Then he pressed deeper, parting her, stroking the silky flesh of
her softness. And Calli's body made her choice.

"You're so hot," he whispered. "And wet." He circled the
bead of her sex. Calli's legs threatened to fold. Just the sight of
them in the mirror, together, his dark hands intimately on her
body, was more erotic than anything she'd ever known. She felt
cherished and sexy. And decadent. Then he sank a finger inside
her and she bit her lower lip, answering the motion of his thrust.
Gabe stroked her, feeling her body grip and flex beneath his
touch. He tipped her head and took her mouth, his kiss slow and
drugging. His knee insinuated itself between hers from behind
and he felt the exquisite heat of her center baring down on him.

He drank in her gasps of pleasure, absorbed her sensations and
lived in them. Her body ripened against him like the blossom of
forbidden fruit. His hardness thickened, throbbed with each subtle
shift of her body as he withdrew and plunged softly.

"Yes," he growled in her ear, watching her body's reflection
undulate in an exotic tempo. "Sweet, so sweet."

She gripped his arm strung across her waist, fingertips digging,
and Gabriel knew she was close. He wanted to feel it, the hot
rush of her pleasure, to know that he gave it to her, could give
to her without taking anything back. Even though he ached to
open his jeans and push inside her body, take her on the dresser
as he'd threatened before. But he wouldn't. She was suddenly so
much more important than his own crushing desire.

He met her gaze in the mirror, saw it slide down to where his
hand lay and he knew it aroused her, aroused him. His groin
pulsed with need and he drove his touch deeper. She cupped his
head and drew him to her mouth, her tongue pushing between his
lips. She ground against him and he answered the push, experi-
encing her explosion as if it were his own; her breath rushing
along his cheek, her body flexing, straining. She whimpered softly
and he stilled, letting her ride the wave of her desire in his arms.
It was several moments before she collapsed against him. Then

slowly, he wrapped her in his arms. The scent of her, like nothing he'd ever known, filled him, lingered on him. Her breathing calmed and he brushed her hair back from her face.

She groaned and turned in his arms, burying her face in the curve of his shoulder.

"But you—" she said, brushing her fingertips to the band of his jeans.

He caught her wrist, imprisoning it against his chest. "I'm okay."

He wasn't, she could tell. His heart was thundering beneath her palm and Calli lifted her gaze to his. She was incredibly aroused, aching for more of him, but she wasn't going to push the issue. Letting him touch her like that was probably the most unwise thing she'd ever done. It took them across that undefinable line in the sand.

Gabe held her gaze and saw apprehension, a little fear. "Get ready for church, tigress," he said before brushing his mouth across hers. "I'll take you to talk with your god."

Then he left and as he disappeared around the doorjamb, Calli knew that last comment came from Angel. He was already regretting touching her.

# Eight

Gabe didn't think he'd seen any woman blush as much as Calli. But every time she met his gaze on the ride here, her face flamed. When she went into the chapel, looking more like a schoolgirl than a world-class chef, it struck him again how different they really were.

Less than an hour later, people filed out, pausing to chat with the priest, then to stare at him where he leaned against his truck. Gabe simply stared straight ahead, his arms folded over his chest. He felt out of place, unwanted. It was a familiar feeling, which is why he kept to his ranch. Yet with Calli here, this was the most he'd been in town in two years.

She stopped short at the sight of him and his gaze combed her electric-blue tank dress and matching sandals. Sweet. Yet it was the blue headband that made her look untouchably innocent, he decided, forbidden. It drew him to her like a magnet.

"Did you confess your sins?" he asked lowly when she was close, stepping back to open the door.

She smiled up at him, laying a hand on his arm. His surroundings seemed to fade to nothing but those bright blue eyes.

"No," she said, her expression deadpan. "I confessed yours."

His brows rose before he sent her a narrow look. "Yeah, right."

She could tell he was unsure. "Suit yourself." She shrugged and climbed into the cab. Her gaze followed him as he walked around the front end and slid behind the wheel. "Now where?"

"I have to head back."

She was disappointed. "It's Sunday, Gabe. Even God rested."

"God wasn't in debt." He stared out over the hood of the black truck. "I wish I could—"

"No problem," she said as he pulled into traffic. "It's too congested anyway." He maneuvered around tourists and locals.

"Don't like crowds?"

She shook her head. "Not especially. I don't get nervous or anything, but I lived in crowds for years. The orphanage was like having three hundred roommates, twenty-four hours a day."

They were headed on the road out of town when Gabe suddenly pulled into a parking lot. Calli leaned out to read the sign. It was a restaurant, a tiny, old-fashioned fifties-style diner, pink and white, lots of chrome.

She looked at him. "What are we doing here?"

Gabe shrugged. "I figured I owed you at least one meal you didn't have to cook."

She smiled, feeling something light flutter in her chest, and waited for him to come around to her side. It wasn't a gallant gesture on his part, opening her door like that, but a protective one. She slid from the seat, brushing close to him.

He stared down at her for a brief moment, his hand rising toward her cheek, then he seemed to shake himself, drop his arm and step back. What kept pushing him away? she wondered as they walked to the entrance. The instant they were inside, the din lessened, a few dozen pairs of eyes linking him to her. A girl in a pink uniform came up to them, her gaze rudely breaking between Calli and her "date." Calli smiled and inched closer to him, but Gabe only stared at the waitress.

"Would you prefer the counter or—"

"A booth, in the back," Gabe said, and the girl blinked, then grabbed two menus from a rack and immediately spun around. Calli looked up at him, trying not to frown. He really ought to be more courteous, she thought, then felt the weight of his palm on the small of her back, guiding her as they followed the waitress to a secluded booth. Sliding into their seats, Gabe accepted the menu without a glance. Calli relaxed back and studied it carefully. Then she studied him over the edge of plastic-coated paper. He was retreating, she could feel it in the way he stared blankly out the window, the hard cast to his handsome features. She nudged him under the table.

"Loosen up, this was your idea."

"I hate crowds."

She set the menu down and leaned close. A crowd to Gabriel was anyone other than himself, yet it was a common thread. And she was going to pull on it. "Now, why is that?"

He shrugged, muscles flexing with the subtle gesture. She briefly let her gaze wander over his thick arms, the tight white T-shirt she knew was tucked into faded blue jeans, no belt. Heavens, the man was beyond sexy. He reeked of it. Good thing he didn't know it.

"More people to stare, I guess."

"If you don't like them staring, you shouldn't have done that." She nodded to his tattooed arms.

"Did them for me," he said with a strange finality, then arched a brow. "Bother you?"

"No." She let her gaze sweep hotly over him. "I think they're intriguing." She'd had a fantasy since she'd seen them, of outlining them with her fingers, then her tongue. But she wasn't going to tell him that. "Tell me when you got them."

"Maybe later." He inclined his head to the approaching waitress, effectively dismissing the conversation. Gabe sat back and watched her. Dining was an art form for her and she was in her element. She didn't act superior or make outrageous requests, but casual inquiries. And she made the waitress feel comfortable, calling her by her name. She ordered, then she and the woman turned their attention to him, waiting.

"The same," he said, handing back the menu without looking, then shifting in the leather booth and propping his arm on the back of the seat. Calli was so damn beautiful his heart clenched just to look at her. And he wanted to do more than just look.

"Gabriel," she whispered. He still stared.

"Yeah."

"You're staring at me."

"So."

"It's the way you're doing it, that's the problem."

His gaze skimmed her body. "I was remembering this morning."

Her cheeks flamed and she adjusted her napkin on her lap. He wondered how many of those blushes he could get from her in one day.

"You are shameless."

He arched a dark brow, his look telling her he knew that.

"And so am I."

He leaned across the table and said in a rough whisper, "Baby, you are the furthest thing from shame I have ever met."

Calli blinked. She didn't know exactly how to take that. A compliment or a challenge. She searched his eyes, trying to read beyond his startlingly pale gaze. "You think I'm such a good girl. Like the nuns who raised me, don't you?"

"You are." He needed to touch her. He didn't know what it was about her, exactly—maybe it was the scooping neckline of her tank dress against her skin, or the way she licked her lips, slowly, as if she knew no one would be noticing but him. Yet his desire to tempt her innocence, to hear her soft breathless rush of rapture, was eating him alive. Suddenly he slid out of his seat and into hers. He was close, so close she could see the length of his lashes, the stitching on his T-shirt, feel the pressure of his thigh against hers. He angled his body toward her, hemming her in, his big shoulders shielding even a glimpse of the crowded restaurant.

"Your seat not good enough?" she said a little breathlessly, inclining her head to the other side of the table.

"The view's better here." His right hand covered her thigh just below the hem of her dress.

"What are you doing?"

"Tempting you."

"This is that good-girl thing, isn't it?" His hand slid subtly beneath her hem. She caught it, covered it with her own. "Gabriel?"

A mischievous smile curved his lips. "Ever been daring, Cal, really daring?" He propped his left forearm on the back of the leather seat, his fingers toying with a lock of her hair, his gaze on his movements. To anyone who looked, they appeared to be having an intimate conversation.

"Of course."

"When?"

"Coming to your ranch," she offered.

"No. I mean outrageous."

He said it like a taunt, a secret. "What are you getting at?" She was almost afraid to find out.

He leaned in a bit closer, his right hand moving higher, the coarse texture of his fingertips stirring over her skin, arousing her. "I remember this morning," he growled in her ear, and she made a weakening sound. "How you felt, inside. It was incredible. I want it again." His fingertips met the apex of her thighs and a flood of moisture dampened her skin. "Open for me, tigress."

Calli swallowed nervously and met his gaze. "No." She couldn't believe he was touching her like this! In public!

"Look around you. No one is watching." Her gaze breezed the crowd. He was right. "So private." His fingertip rode up the thin fabric of her panties. "Yet so public."

"Gabriel."

He made a hissing sound. "I like when you say my name like that, all breathy and deep." He could feel the moist heat of her and tempted her across the line between playing it safe...and taking risks. "Open for me." His hand nudged her and without thought she complied, his touch branding her. Then he hooked the side of her panties and deftly slipped a finger between the soft, dewy folds.

Calli gasped, tensed.

"No, don't move. Look at me," he told her, and she did. He stroked her, gently introducing another finger and pushing deeper, his thumb circling the delicate bead of her sex. Feminine flesh gripped and flexed. "I can feel you wanting me," he whispered. "In a roomful of people you're too aroused to fight it. Do you know what that does to me?"

Calli briefly closed her eyes, her hand slipping to his leg. She squeezed. A muscle flexed in his jaw. She knew what it did. The evidence of his need strained against his jeans, against her touch.

The waitress brought their drinks, setting them on the table. Calli lifted her gaze to the girl. The waitress smiled tightly, cast a quick look at the back of Gabe's head, then left.

"See?" He deepened his touch, quickened it. She bit back a moan. "Shh," he whispered. "Laugh."

"I can't," came her pant. Her blood rushed in her ears, thoughts too crowded to even consider thinking. Dishes clattered, people called out, laughed, a child cried somewhere in the recesses of the restaurant, but Calli's world narrowed to the man beside her, his fingers stroking over her most private area in a very public place. It was erotic, exciting, and ultimately the most daring thing she'd ever done. Like getting away with a crime.

"Look at me." She held his gaze as he stroked her. His breathing was harsh, his features tight with unclaimed need. "I want to taste you there, hold you against me and feel you ride my mouth." She moaned, tight and clipped. "Let it go, tigress." Then it happened, her body sang, throbbed, and he pushed and pushed. She curled toward him, grasping the band of his jeans with both hands. Her lips parted, a soft shudder spilling from her lips and into his mouth. He drank it, the dampness of her breath whispering over his lips. A near kiss.

She inhaled short, quick breaths, and his touch lessened, holding her on the edge of completion for several moments. His gaze searched hers, pale and sparkling and pleased. Then she sank, into him, into the seat.

"Sweet," he said softly, curling the words around his tongue. Calli loosened her grip on his waistband and closed her eyes. A rush of color filled her cheeks. He chuckled lowly and her skin fused darker.

Slowly he removed his hand and used the napkin lying across her lap. His gaze caressed her as he inhaled through clenched teeth. "Outrageous."

Calli swallowed, took a hasty sip of her drink, then lifted her gaze. "Dangerous," she corrected.

He pressed his lips to her temple and beneath the guard of the tablecloth, his hand slid over her stomach and caressed her hip. "Want to do it again?"

She tipped her head back to look at him, studying him briefly. "You're serious," came a tiny shriek.

"I've touched you." A pause and then, "Now I want to taste you."

She choked and Gabe chuckled darkly and decided it was time to give her a break. He shifted out of her seat and into his. He let out a soft groan as he sat.

"Hurt?"

His gaze sharpened on her. His lips quirked. "What do you think?"

"I think you are paying the price of your own behavior." There was smugness in her tone he found intriguing.

"I'll get over it."

He was in pain. He had to be. She'd felt the hard length of his arousal when she'd gripped his jeans. It had practically burned her. Calli tried mustering up some dignity when all she could think of was how they'd spent the last few moments. One of these days, she thought, she would have to find the nerve to pay him back in spades.

The waitress returned, sliding their orders in front of them.

"Calli, what is this?" His gaze shifted between the plates.

"Food." He gave her an impatient smile and she wondered how he could dismiss what they'd just done so easily. Her body was still humming. "Poached eggs in flour crepes, hash browns with onions and mushrooms, and a side of sausage." She picked up her fork and speared her crepe. "All for the startlingly low price of five ninety-five." She sampled it. Her smile fell, her eyes widening.

His chuckle was soft. "Tastes like it, too, huh?"

She chewed and swallowed, then gulped her drink. "Good grief, it's salty!" she sputtered, then valiantly took a bite of the hash browns. It was just as bad. And they went downhill from there. She set aside her fork and lifted her gaze to his. Gabe, wisely, had not touched his lunch.

"Sorry."

"Not your fault," he told her, his lips twitching.

She glanced around. "How can business be so good, if the food is so bad?" The place was packed.

"I think they do burgers and fries better than this." He nodded to his untouched plate.

Calli inclined her head to the side. "Ready to blow this joint?"

Gabe smiled, slid from the seat and tossed a few bills onto the table. Her eyes wouldn't obey and she lowered to the front of his jeans.

"Oh, my." His gaze flashed to hers, a crooked smile ghosting his lips. "Can you walk?"

Her skin pinkened and he laughed. It brought heads around. But it was still very obvious he was aroused. Calli grabbed his hand and, using her body to shield him, they headed out. The waitress froze in the center aisle, her hands full of steaming plates as they passed her.

"Something wrong, Mr. Griffin?"

"Nothing you can fix," he muttered. Outside, she stopped, her hands on his biceps as she tipped her head back to look at him. Then in the full light of half the town, he kissed her, the hot force of his mouth burning over her lips. The contact was like the ignition of jet fuel. A flash of fire and heat. Unfinished desire and the need for satisfaction blazed, and he groaned deeply, dragging her tightly against him, his mouth slanting savagely back and forth over hers.

Calli felt his hands ride heavily up her back, fist in her clothes, in her body, as if to push her into his skin. His kiss was utterly possessive, devouring, and Calli had the distinct feeling he was staking his claim. When he pulled back, her lips were numb and he was breathing hard. She was as stunned as he.

"Wow." They spoke in unison.

Slowly he let her go, a funny grin brightening his features. But just as quickly it faded. He stared somewhere behind her and she followed the direction of his gaze. A man in ragged clothing stood off to the side of the diner on the edge of the lot.

"Spare some change, mister?"

Gabe fished for his wallet, but it was empty. He cursed, then quickly scrounged in his pockets, pulling out a crumpled dollar bill, crossing to hand it to the old man. "Wish it was more, pal," he said softly, and Calli recognized the sincerity in his voice. Would she ever understand this man?

Gabe faced her, frowning softly. She had a peculiar look on her face, as if she'd just discovered something odd. He was about to ask her about it when she walked to the truck.

Calli kept her thoughts to herself and climbed into the cab. "Someone needs to teach you the fine art of selecting a restaurant."

Gabe backed out of the parking lot, his gaze in the rearview mirror. "Someone needs to teach their chef what real cooking is."

"Did you do that on purpose? Choose such a rotten place that I would be forced to cook this afternoon?"

His head snapped around. "No! I've only been in there once or twice."

"Chill out, Gabe, I was just teasing. And I hope all you *ever* did in there was eat."

"Food, yes."

"Gabriel," she scolded, and that raspy chuckle came again. She liked hearing it, loved his smile, even if they were just little ones. She cast a look out the back window at the diner. "But I really would like to know how that place stays in operation with such lousy cuisine."

"Great place to have under-the-table sex?" he offered.

"Gabriel!"

He grinned, winking at her, and Calli sank into the seat. She laughed softly to herself, shaking her head. She still couldn't believe she'd allowed such a thing. But it was good, she thought, feeling wicked and sexy. So good. Working off her sandals, she propped her feet on the dusty dash, wiggling her painted toes.

Gabe almost went off the rode twice just staring at her bare legs. As he drove, he nudged a large paper sack toward her. Calli arched a tapered brow.

"For you," was all he said. He'd never given anyone anything before. What if she didn't like it?

She grabbed the sack and opened it, peering inside.

"Well, you've been busy this morning. How did you find these?"

He shrugged, noncommittally, but the pleasure on her face made him indescribably happy.

Calli hugged the bagful of fresh peaches and coconuts. It was better than receiving diamonds. That he'd remembered and hunted them down told her more about him than words. She leaned over, clutching the bag to her chest, then gripped his arm to pull him close. She brushed a kiss to his cheek.

"Thank you, Gabriel." He thought he heard a catch in her voice, but wasn't sure. Then he dismissed it as she sighed deeply and closed her eyes. The contentment on her face wrenched his heart. It wouldn't last and he knew she expected him to take more from her. That wasn't going to happen. It would just magnify the lie he was living. He didn't deserve to have her in his bed the way he wanted, the way he'd dreamed of since he'd first clapped eyes on her. And he could never have her in his life permanently. He hated himself for even thinking further than today. He was a selfish, lying bastard and he wanted more than just combustible sex with sweet Calli Thornton. Yet, he was willing to experience her passion as often as he could, give only to her, before he went completely mad. That would be a fitting price for lying to her. And he really didn't deserve even that.

"Son of a bitch!"

"What?" she said, sitting up and blinking as they pulled onto the drive. She inhaled. "The gate's open!"

"I know." Regret filled his voice.

The truck raced up the drive. Gabe cursed again.

The colt was gone.

# Nine

Gabe slammed on the brakes, threw the gear into park and was out of the truck before Calli knew what was happening.

The corral was empty and she knew both mother and child were gone. And that someone had to have let them out. There were no tire tracks, no breakage on the fence or locks.

"Who would have done such a thing?"

"Could be one of several," he muttered as he stormed into the barn, checking the other mounts and finding them unharmed.

Damn. Dave Rubeck was going to think he'd sold off his horse and the colt. Hell, he'd had to talk fast and deal to get him to offer him the foal in the first place. Even though the mare was trail quality, the colt was sired by a decent Thoroughbred. Gabe had seen it as his only chance to gain some stock of his own. He muttered a curse and drew a gelding from the stall, immediately throwing on a blanket. He was lifting the saddle onto the mount's back when Calli came into the barn.

"I'm sorry."

It was the sound of her voice that made him look up.

He cursed again, dropping the saddle and coming to her, tipping her head back. A lone tear skated down her cheek.

"Aw, hell, Cal, don't cry." He could face losing his ranch better than her tears.

"This is my fault." She crunched the paper bag of peaches and coconuts in her fist.

His brows drew down. "How you figure?"

"If I hadn't wanted to stay in town, you wouldn't have felt guilty and taken me into the restaurant. We might have been here before anything could have happened."

"This has nothing to do with you."

She shrugged, but Gabe didn't think she believed him. "You're going to look."

"They can't be too far."

She nodded and turned away. He went back to saddling the horse.

"We should call the police," she said.

"No!"

She turned back to look at him, frowning. "Gabe, someone did this to you, intentionally."

"I know."

"Why? And don't tell me it's your enemies."

No, he thought, it's yours. Whoever did this knew he would go looking for the mare and colt, and that he wouldn't leave Calli behind alone. But her suitcase and journal would be. It was a lame cover-up.

"Just don't call anyone," he warned.

Involving the police meant telling Calli why she was really here and fessing up to his lies. He didn't want her gone, just yet. He couldn't even let the thought enter his head right now. He was in deep trouble on that score. But he wasn't about to let someone else stick their nose in his affairs and he would be damned if he would allow her to find out this way. Gabe wondered if he would ever have the guts to tell her what he'd done. Unable to look her in the eye, he turned away and finished saddling the horse.

*Fine, keep your damn secrets*, Calli thought as she left the barn.

"Don't go inside just yet," he said, and when she didn't respond, he turned.

He cursed, heading to the house in a dead run. He called her name, once, twice, then frantically when she didn't answer right away.

She poked her head out her bedroom door. "Good grief, Gabe, I'm right here."

He sagged against the door frame, shoving his hand through his hair. He wouldn't look at her just yet, afraid of what he'd do if he crossed the room and touched her.

"All right, Griffin, what's going on?" She filled the doorway, tucking her shirt into black jeans.

Gabe looked around his house. Everything was in its place. "I thought whoever let the colt loose might be in here."

Calli's harsh expression faded to a tender smile. For all his abruptness, his rough edges, inside, Gabe Griffin was a marshmallow. And he cared. A lot more than he let on. "Faker. Faker, faker," she crooned like a kid.

He looked at her and arched one brow.

"You aren't so tough, Gabriel." She crossed to him. "And I can take care of myself, you know."

He scoffed gently. "You're a shrimp."

She shrugged and darted back into her room for her jacket.

"Any signs that someone was in your room?"

"No." Why would they? she thought. No one knew she was here. "And I don't have anything left to steal." She breezed past him out the door. "Except a few lace panties," she taunted.

Gabe caught her arm.

She rolled her eyes. "Get that smirk off your face. It's evil."

Gabe chuckled to himself, then his features hardened. "That book, ah, journal. Better lock it in the car."

"It already is."

He nodded, thinking it was going to be harder to search through it if he needed the key to get past her car alarms. God, he was no better than the creep who'd let loose his colt, he thought, locking up the house.

He tipped his head to look at her. "You ever ridden a horse?"

"Yes," she said too quickly as she stepped under the porch, dragging bread and cold cuts from the fridge. She was not going to be left behind, neither would she admit that yes, she had sat on a horse. A pony. At a church carnival. She was likely the only Texan who couldn't ride. What could be so difficult?

"We don't have time for that." He gestured to the sandwich she was cutting.

She didn't look up as she wrapped it neatly and started another. "Go saddle up, cowboy." That made her smile and she could almost feel him scowling at her. "If I'm not ready by the appointed time, you can leave without me."

Gabe wasn't about to let her out of his sight and hurried into the barn to saddle a horse for her.

Calli went into overdrive, grabbing up a burlap sack still holding a few apples and adding some more fruit to go with the sandwiches. She was juggling the sack and tying her jacket around her waist when he led the horses out of the barn. Calli refused to show her apprehension as she tied the sack to the pommel and with as much courage as she could, swung up into the saddle. Gabe did the same and glanced back.

"Oh, my lord," she muttered under her breath. The ground looked too far away.

Gabe hid a smile, then focused on the terrain. The canyon was rough and hilly, but he knew the horses would head to water. He had already scanned the area with binoculars and now they had to climb the ridge above the canyon.

Calli followed, bouncing along, and it was a good two hours of vicious riding before she realized that rising up with the jolt of the horse would ease the pain in her rear. She was praying feverishly that they would find the horses, soon, when Gabe called to her, rather loudly.

"You okay?"

"Sure, sure," she said absently. "Praying."

He eased back till he was beside her, yet his gaze raked the land. "Always the good girl, huh?"

She scoffed. "I haven't been under the supervision of nuns since I was seventeen. A lot has happened."

"Such as?"

"Beyond this morning?"

He chuckled.

"You don't want to hear it."

AMY FETZER                                    133

"Wouldn't ask, Cal."

She eyed him. His expression revealed nothing, but she could read the curiosity in his gaze. It was as if he didn't want to admit he wanted to know. But if she told him, would he simply compare her to him and find himself lacking?

"When I was about two my mother set me on the steps of the orphanage with a paper sack of clothes, a note pinned to my jacket and told me to stay put." She tore her gaze from his and stared at the reins in her hands. "And I did, all night, in the cold until the sisters opened the gates."

"You didn't cry out? Call to someone?"

Her gaze flew to his. "Why? The only one I wanted was my mother and she drove away with her stereo blaring."

Gabe's heart clenched in his chest as he imagined the abandoned little girl. The woman beside him was so far removed from the picture she painted.

"I was fostered off several times and always sent back."

His brow lifted a fraction.

"Not many people want a rebellious two-year-old, let alone a ten-year-old or twelve or...well, you get the picture."

"You stayed there."

"I had nowhere else to go, except to the streets, and I wasn't brave enough for that." She pulled a ball cap from her back pocket, unfolding it. "I always wondered what kind of person would invite a child into their home and then when they got a little troublesome, send them back like an underdone steak."

He could hear the pain in her voice, even though she tried to hide it. It was something he excelled at. "Some just don't care enough."

She nodded, agreeing, and even though the sisters welcomed her back, insisting they missed her, Calli could never escape the feeling that there had been something wrong with her that her own mother and those prospective parents all saw. Sometimes, that awful feeling surfaced, but Calli faced long ago that there was no use dwelling on it. She liked herself and that was all that mattered.

"It's a fault they have to live with, not me. I forgave them anyway,'' she said, and as she shoved her hair back and put on the cap, Gabe stared at her, hard, as if he couldn't believe her.

Then Gabe read the writing on her cap and busted out with laughter.

"What?" she said annoyed as she adjusted the cap. Mercy, her behind hurt.

He pointed to the cap, toning his laugh down to a snicker. "'Betty Crocker Bake-Off,' Cal? Figures."

She leaned over and gave him a shove. "Don't knock it, Gabriel. The cash I won put me through my first year at the Culinary Institute."

That sobered him. Cooking was more lucrative than he thought and he didn't want to know how much money this woman made making everyone's taste buds dance.

"So," she said, folding her arms, her look patient. "What about you?"

"I'm hungry."

Her lips pulled into a tight line and she slung the sack at him. He caught it, rummaging. A minute later, he bit into a sandwich and when she pestered him again, he said it wasn't polite to talk with his mouth full and kept eating. Avoidance, she decided, was Gabriel Griffin's finest talent. And it was really starting to tick her off.

Fine. She knew when to catch him.

She took a sandwich when he offered it and ate, her hips rolling with the gate of the horse and Gabe let his gaze drop to her thighs spread wide over the mount. He wanted to be between them. Damn, couldn't he look at her without thinking about making love to her?

*Making love,* the words whispered through his brain. He could honestly say he'd never done that with a woman. Sex, yes. But love? He wasn't capable of loving someone, so the matter was insignificant. He cast another look at her and she reached across to brush crumbs from his shirt. Her every gesture was giving and caring and he soaked it up like a sponge, sitting still when she rubbed her thumb over the corner of his mouth to remove a smudge of mustard. God, he was going to miss her when she was gone.

A heaviness swelled in his chest, bruising against his heart, and Gabe had to look away and remember to breathe. His fingers flexed on the reins. Damn.

He handed her the sack, then kicked the horse into a brisk cantor and headed up the ridge, glancing back to see if she was still there. She was, bouncing on the saddle like one of those balls suspended by a rubber band from a paddle. He reined in, waiting for her to catch up, and smothered a grin. She was cursing and gripping the pommel for dear life.

His ears pricked to sound and Gabe twisted in the saddle, leather creaking. His gaze sharpened on the terrain, then he angled the horse farther up the rise. A stream gurgled back down through the canyon walls and his pulse picked up speed as he crested the top. He sighed with relief. Mother and colt were side by side, drinking. He loosened a pair of ropes as he slipped from the saddle, then motioned to Calli to stay back. He eased closer.

He swung the rope over his head, quick, soundless.

Calli was stunned as he crept carefully closer, then snapped his wrist and sent the rope around the mare's neck. She inhaled as the colt bolted, racing erratically, so pitifully confused, but Gabe ran and caught her gently around the throat with the second rope. Amazing. He checked their legs, running his broad hands over their stockings, and his shoulders fell with relief. She wished he would care about her that much. Heck, she wished he would take her in his arms and make wild love to her right here in the dirt. But he wouldn't. She didn't know how she knew that for certain, but she did. *He gives and never takes,* she thought. And if she'd press the issue he'd claim himself too harsh, too jaded, for someone like her. She hated being a good girl and wished she had the nerve to be really bad and tempt him into her bed.

Calli swung from the saddle and promptly landed in the dirt. She moaned, tears bursting in her eyes. She quickly rethought that making-love-in-the-dirt thing and rubbed her abused behind.

Gabe looked up and forced back a smile. Drawing the horse from the stream, he tied the leads to his saddle and came around to Calli. His hands on his hips, he gazed down at the woman in the dirt.

"Never ridden, have you?"

"How could you tell?" she snapped. She hadn't looked at him and his forehead wrinkled as he bent to help her up. "I'm fine!" She batted away his hand and struggled to her feet. Her legs were the consistency of pudding with lumps and she grit her teeth as she straightened to her full, all-imposing five foot four.

"Why didn't you say something? I wouldn't have ridden so hard or so long without a break."

She cast him a glance from beneath the brim of her cap. "Didn't want you to think I was a wimp."

"I never thought that." His lips quirked with a rascally grin that said otherwise.

"Right. I know what you think. Betty Crocker, Goody Two-shoes, a novitiate to the convent San Tanco, take your pick!"

Calli didn't know what was wrong with her that a hot bath wouldn't fix and she walked carefully to the water. She didn't sit, that would hurt too much, but she was, however, tempted to strip and go for a swim. She heard him come up behind her.

"We have to go back before it gets too dark."

He didn't lay a hand on her, not that she wouldn't let him. He excited her, just the thought of him so near, the sound of his breathing. His scent. Calli wanted things she couldn't have from him. For him to take her in his arms, tell her he loved her and surrender to this insatiable fire between them. But that wasn't going to happen. Just like everything else, no matter how long she stayed here with him, how many times they were intimate, he wasn't going to open up to her because he thought she was too tenderhearted to hear the gory details. She didn't *need* to hear them. It was just that those details were keeping him from her when she wanted him close. Face facts, she thought. Gabriel Griffin wasn't the tie-down-and-love-forever kind of man and she had known that going in. It didn't make her feel any better about wishing for more, though.

Calli looked at the water, aching to take off her clothes and tease him until he couldn't do anything *but* make love to her. Yet in her present mood, that would be for all the wrong reasons. She wanted something from him and not just his hand up her skirt.

She turned away and climbed back into the saddle, gritting back a moan.

He gazed up at her. She looked ready to bolt or throw something at him. "What's going on?"

"You tell me, Gabriel. I could lay out my past in a neat little block for you, but other than a little risky business in a restaurant, what have you really offered that I didn't have to pull from you like teeth?"

Defensive anger lit his features, making him look volatile. "What the hell brought this on?"

"My sore pride, I suppose." She stared out over the scenery. He recognized the look in her eyes. Pain, distance.

Couldn't she just take it like it was, he thought. "What do you want from me?"

"Nothing, except some honesty, for God's sake!"

That bit into him like the slice of a blade. He wasn't being honest. He was flat-out lying to her. And it angered him that he'd let this incurable need for her in his life, even for just a little while, drag her heart through the mud. "What would satisfy you, Calli? Huh?" he said like a taunt, anger building. "How about that I was so unwanted my parents dumped me in a trash can at Yankee Stadium!"

Calli couldn't look more stunned.

"Happy?" he snarled, then strode back to the stream, cupping his hands and taking a drink.

Dismounting, she moved beside him, crouching. It was an open door and she nudged it wider. "Go on, Gabriel."

He ran his wet hands through his hair. God, he didn't want to do this. "The janitor found me, took me home, raised me till I was about five or six." His brows drew down with the memory, his gaze on the brook. "I came home from my first day of school and found him dead."

Calli inhaled, thinking of a small boy finding a dead body and losing his innocence in one brutal blow. "My Lord, Gabe." Her eyes burned. "How?"

He chucked a rock into the stream. "Shot." He slid her a glance and noticed her glossy eyes. "Cleaning the stadium wasn't his only profession."

Her eyes widened. "Drugs?"

"Took me a while to figure that one out, but, yeah."

"Didn't the police take you to welfare?"

His next words came on a short, caustic laugh. "Didn't even know I existed. I hid out."

"Why did you do that?"

He rubbed the back of his neck. "Hell, I don't know! Scared I guess."

"Then what?"

He straightened and so did she. "Then nothing, Cal. I was alone."

"You mean you were on the streets at six?" she whispered.

"Wasn't that hard," he rasped bitterly. "Street folk take care of their own."

He stared off to the side and she stepped closer, her body brushing his as she forced him to look at her. A muscle ticked in his jaw. His pale gaze blistered over her face.

He waited for her pity and it didn't come.

"And you're ashamed of this?" Her voice rose in pitch. "My Lord—" she brushed his dark hair from his forehead "—you're lucky to be alive."

"Yeah, real lucky." Hostile, wounded.

She blinked, dropping her hands. Then she drew back her fist and socked him in the arm.

"Ow," he said, deadpan.

"You are so damn...blind."

That irritating eyebrow rose.

"You can't even see what's in front of you." She poked his chest, shoving him back with every word. "A home, land, food, a place to work. A place to belong." She was in his face, her body pushing against his, her eyes glinting like blue fire and all Gabe could think was, *Magnificent.* "You, Mr. Griffin—" she fisted his shirtfront "—need a lesson in simple gratitude." She clipped the back of his knee with her heel and he went down with a grunt. She loomed over him, her heel pressing into his solar plexus as she ticked off on her fingers all he should remember.

"Never take anything or anyone for granted, Gabriel. Be thankful for what you have, because it could easily vanish. Forgive the world and live *your* life in the here and now, not the *then.*" She leaned down into his stunned face and even as he gasped for the breath he couldn't get, she patted his cheek. "And believe a woman when she says she can take care of herself."

She removed her foot, stepping back, and he coughed once, then rose to tower over her. She met his blistering gaze, daring him to unleash his temper on her.

When she looked to explode all over him, he put up his hands in surrender. "I am sufficiently grateful to breathe again, Cal, honest. Trust me."

"I do." He smiled, tender and light, and she tipped her head to the side, unsure. "Focus on the things you can change, Gabe, and let go of the things you can't."

He wasn't going to tell her that was next to impossible since he *was* lying, it *was* something he could change, *if* he wanted to break a client confidentiality. And he had so little honor left, he couldn't. "That your personal philosophy?"

She shook her head. "Sister Mary Margaret's, after I burned her habit."

He chuckled, then took a step away. But she grabbed his arm and after a moment, he looked at her.

Her voice was infinitely compassionate and low as she said, "They *were* worthless for abandoning you, Gabriel. You're innocent, like I was. Forgive them, thirty years is a long time to hate someone. Especially when they don't know it."

Suddenly, Gabe gathered her into his arms and she laid her head on his chest. "How did you get so wise?" he whispered, shaping her back with his broad hands.

She moved her shoulders. "Born a woman, I guess."

A ghost of a smile toyed at his lips as he pressed them to the top of her head. He gazed out over the horizon. A dark, greedy hunger ignited and burned in his chest.

Her words played over and over in his mind in a confusing circle, yet one thought came back to him, pounding his bruised heart and making him ache for Calli in a way he'd never thought possible.

*Will she forgive me so easily?*

Gabe closed his eyes and for the first time in years, allowed himself to hope for the impossible.

# Ten

Calli eyed him as they walked down the well-lit street past shops. He knew who'd let the horses loose and he was here to find them. Why she was along, she didn't know, but as soon as they'd locked up the horses and changed clothes, he'd called Bull from her car phone to come safeguard the ranch. Then he'd herded her into the truck, driving without talking. Three times tonight, he'd left her standing off to the side while he spoke to some less-than-reputable-looking people, then came back to her and continued walking.

She knew he wouldn't tell her whom he suspected. Or why.

Suddenly he tensed and she followed the direction of his gaze. She didn't see anyone.

"Go inside." He nodded to the drugstore.

"Gabe?" She looked up at him, worried.

He pressed a soft kiss to her forehead and murmured, "I'll be back. Trust me." He stuffed the truck keys into her hand, then left her, an uneasy feeling brushing up her spine. She watched him vanish around the side of a building, then she obeyed and stepped into the drugstore.

Gabriel pressed his back against the wall, knee bent, foot braced on the brick. His eyes narrowed dangerously and a passer-by hastened his pace, crossing the street to avoid him. Gabe scarcely noticed, his gaze on the man conversing with a couple of well-known hoods outside a restaurant just a few feet away. Though they looked like anyone else, a little touristy even, the gray limo was hard to miss. If he wanted discretion, Gabe thought cynically, he should have hired him. He waited until the precise moment that Murdock noticed him. Murdock's eyes widened. He shoved a flunky back and scrambled to get into his limo. Gabe pushed away from the wall and raced toward him.

He didn't say a word as he reached for him, grabbing him by the arm and dragging him nearly off his feet to meet his face. His pals, likely fresh out on parole, split like scattering mice. Gabriel grinned, a slow baring of white teeth.

Murdock swallowed.

"Come near my place and you're a dead man."

Murdock rustled a little courage and snickered, yanking his arm free. "You have no idea what you've got, do you?"

Gabe arched a single brow.

"Excalibur is the best of the best. One creation is a gold mine."

Though Murdock's eyes brightened with excitement, Gabe remained silent, his features impassive.

"Don't look so pious. I know about you, Angel," Murdock said with a disgusted snicker. "Your past record proves you're not an all-American do-gooder. That private investigator license is just a handy inside track when the right job comes along, huh?"

Gabe's fists clenched. He knew Murdock was leading up to something. "Spill it."

"She's in your house, right? Get her winter line for me, and I'll make it worth your time." Gabe's gaze sharpened. "From the looks of your ranch, you could use the cash. And she's hot-looking. Soften her up." Murdock grinned, a slimy twist of his lips, then unwisely gave Gabe a shove. "Just screw her a few times, if you haven't already."

"You're a pig, Murdock."

Murdock shrugged, unaffected. "A rich one. You could be, too."

"Forget it."

The chauffeur came out of the restaurant, then dashed toward them and Gabe instantly sensed Murdock's sudden gust of bravery. Murdock swung. Gabe blocked it, then did something he'd swore he wouldn't. He drove his fist into Murdock's face, bone shifting under the force. The man's eyes rolled, blood seeped from his nose. His back hit the car. Gabe shook his hand, then faced the chauffeur. The man froze, throwing his hands up as Murdock grappled for balance and failed, sliding down the side of the limo to the ground.

Gabe leaned down, his voice dark with deadly promise. "Like I said, touch what's mine and you're a dead man."

Murdock clutched his bleeding nose and waved, understanding. Gabe walked away, fury still singing through him. He couldn't call in a favor and have Murdock arrested. He had no proof, only running on instinct and the word of a few snitches. What if she'd been there when they had? They would have roughed her up till she'd given them her journal. She would have, he thought, and then where would Daniel be? Daniel, the one man who'd put his faith in Gabe, would be ruined. He quickened his steps, the only thought racing through his head was that he needed to hold Calli.

Calli strolled, pretending to shop, her gaze flicking between the door and the wide windows. Her palms sweat and minutes ticked by. Where was he? Was he hurt? The P.A. system crackled and Calli flinched as the manager announced they were closing. Distractedly, she bought a roll of mints, noticing her cash supply was nearly gone. A courier would deliver her traveler's checks to the post office tomorrow, she thought reassuringly. She walked toward the door, opening the roll and cramming mint after mint into her mouth. Her tongue burned and she nearly choked when he appeared at the door.

Relief swept her and she reached. He yanked her into his arms and for a moment, held her, crushing her against him, then tucked her close to his side. They left. Outside, he flung his arm around her shoulder and she wrapped one around his waist. It was comfortable, natural. She could get used to this.

"What did you do?" They walked slowly and she inspected

him from head to foot. He looked fine, a little breathless, but she wanted that to be because he was so close to her.

"Nothing."

"Gabriel," she muttered as people strolled past. "You were fighting."

"No, I wasn't." His look was as innocent as a man with the nickname of Angel could get.

She wasn't fooled and caught his right hand, holding it up. His knuckles were red. She gave him an impatient look.

"It was just a warning."

"How do you know this person was the one who let the horses out?"

He stopped and stared down at her and couldn't tell her his sources had informed him. That he'd suspected Murdock was still around and when Gabe had seen him leave the restaurant across the street, he'd had to clarify a few things.

"He confessed."

"Before or after you punched him?"

"Will you believe me when I say it was self-defense?"

"Yes," came without hesitation. That she trusted his word gave Gabe a strange feeling in the vicinity of his heart. "Now relax," she said as her hand moved over his chest, fingers mapping the hard indentations. Her touch, he decided, would never relax him. "I know just the thing to do it." Suddenly she wiggled out from under his arm, grabbed his hand and pulled him toward a movie theater. She slapped the last of her cash on the counter for tickets and when he looked as if he would fight her, she wiggled her brows and whispered, "We can neck."

His grin said he would hold her to that.

"Popcorn's on you, though, I'm completely broke till tomorrow."

Gabe shelled out for whatever she wanted and, juggling buckets of popcorn and a couple of sodas, she chose the perfect seat, in the back in the dark. The movie started. Gabe could have cared less. He couldn't remember the last time he'd been in a theater, and in the shadows and lights of the screen, he stared at her. She was like a kid, eating popcorn with gusto, sipping her drink.

"You're staring again," she said without looking at him.

"If your hand misses that bucket again, I'll do more than stare."

She looked at him, smiling in the dark, and she leaned closer, catching his hand and drawing his arm around her shoulder. She tipped her head, cupped his strong jaw and kissed him.

He groaned darkly and her hand slid down his chest to the band of his jeans, then lower. She cupped the hard length of him hidden in faded blue denim, fingertips shaping him, and Gabe ground his teeth and caught her wrist, pulling her hand back up. He distracted her by deepening his kiss, his tongue circling the shape of her lips, then plunging deep inside. She moaned softly, a tiny purr, and Gabe thought he'd never heard such an arousing sound. Calli's pleasure was his only thought. He kissed her, pouring the feelings he suppressed when he first spotted Murdock, heard the bastard talk about her like she was some roadhouse tramp. He'd wanted to pound the man into the gravel right there, but then he thought of this woman and he'd calmed. Just her image redirected his anger and Gabe tightened his hold and kissed her and kissed her, his desire multiplying, his mouth a hard slash across hers. The arm of the chair was the only thing keeping her from crawling onto his lap.

"I haven't necked in a theater since I was seventeen," she said, pulling back for a breath.

"I've never done it." He nibbled at her neck, his hand on her bare thigh where her yellow skirt rode up.

"Oooh, a virgin, huh? That's something." Her fingers sank into his hair. A couple a few rows down told them to hush. And Gabe smiled against her mouth, stealing a quick kiss before letting her relax back into her seat. Her breathing was harsh and short and he knew she was trying not to look at him.

Gabe liked that. That she was as weak for him as he was for her. He let his gaze wander over her tank shirt printed with tiny white flowers on yellow, to the hip-hugging skirt and tanned legs. Without looking, he knew her toes were painted. She was incredibly feminine, he thought, yet unintentionally. It was an allure all by itself. Shifting in his seat, he focused on the movie, aching to taste more than her mouth. The bulge in his jeans strained and

Gabe swore softly. Calli laughed, a tiny satisfied sound, and he nudged her.

When the movie ended, Gabe was in no better shape than before. As they left the theater, she paused and nodded to the rest room. Gabe waited and she came out in less than a minute, a light flush to her skin. A mischievous glint in her eyes. She was up to something. He wrapped his arm around her, smiling at her, then a couple of attendants. Hesitantly, they smiled back. Gabe drew Calli tightly against him. He was happy, and it surprised the hell out of him.

"Home?"

That struck him as odd, that she would say that. Home. He never thought he would hear a woman call his run-down dirt ranch "home."

"Yeah." He kissed her for it, for making him feel good inside, deep inside, for the first time in years. He liked the feeling, didn't want to lose its headiness by thinking beyond this instance. They were in the truck and tooling out of town in minutes. It was pitch-black, the moon the only glow on the long drive toward the ranch.

Calli was close to him, but not touching. He forced himself to focus on the road, but she smelled sweet and he was aware of every inch of her compact body beside him. He imagined her in his bed, naked and plush and damp with sweat, calling his name in that breathless way she did when she was aroused. His groin throbbed painfully. Then she touched his arm, sliding her hand to his wrist, pulling it from the wheel. He glanced at her and expected her to loop it around her shoulders.

Instead, she brought his hand to her thigh.

"Cal?"

"Ever done anything daring, Gabe?" she whispered. Her seductive tone made him ache.

He stole another glance. And she pushed his hand deeper beneath her skirt.

And Gabe touched her softness. She was naked.

He choked and slammed on the brakes, angling the truck to the side of the road. He gripped the wheel, breathing heavy. She threw the gear into park and turned off the engine. The silence was crisp with tension.

"Calli, don't do this."

He felt raw and hungry. He couldn't take it. That was why she was in and out of the rest room so quickly. She'd intended to do this. Good Lord. If he'd known she'd walked within two feet of him without a stitch on underneath he would have found the nearest alley and taken her. Fast and quick. A hot tremor racked through him and Gabe didn't think he had the strength left to breathe or speak. Her shadow flickered against the windshield and he felt rather than saw her crawl to her knees. Still he didn't move, didn't look at her. He was going to snap in two if he did.

She grasped his hand and drew it beneath her skirt, between her thighs, letting him feel how wet and hot she was.

Oh, no, Gabe thought. He was going to come apart.

She pushed into his fingers and called his name.

Gabe twisted and fell back against the door. She scooted closer, her hands riding up his thighs from his knees and covering his hardness. The air locked in his lungs. She shaped him, outlining him with a deep, hungry touch. Then she loosened a button.

"What are you doing to me, Cal?"

"Tempting you over the edge," she whispered.

Gabe grit his teeth and gripped the back of the seat. The sound of his zipper opening mixed with his hard breathing. He should stop her, but he couldn't.

"Look at me," she called softly, and he did, slowly lifting his gaze to hers. She slipped her hand inside his jeans. He was bare and she filled her palm with his warmth.

"Oh, Gabriel," she breathed. "You're so hard for me."

He looked at her from hooded eyes. "Baby, I'm always hard for you."

Satisfaction curved her mouth as she slid her fingers over the smooth tip of him. He inhaled sharply, his hands snaking out to catch her wrists and hold her back. Her gaze lowered to his open jeans, to his arousal barely visible. She brought her gaze to his.

"Tell me you want me as much as I do you, Gabriel."

He swallowed thickly.

The air crackled.

Then it exploded.

He suddenly dragged her to him, covering her mouth with his.

His kiss was hot and driving, hungry and seething with weeks of suppressed passion. They groped for each other, her hands diving beneath his shirt, pushing it up, his hands under her skirt, grinding her heat to his. He shifted from behind the wheel and she straddled his thighs. He kissed her and kissed her, driving his hands up her back, beneath her shirt, her bra, pushing fabric out of his way and free of her. Then his mouth was on her skin, her breasts, his hand shaping one mound as his lips sought the hardened tip of the other.

"Gabriel," she panted, her hips rocking as he licked and nipped at her plump breasts, raked his teeth over the soft underside, then drew one hard peak deep into the heat of his mouth. He sucked, his tongue circling, and he gave attention to its mate until she was heaving and damp. His fingertips dug into her buttocks as he pushed her down against his arousal. Her hands were wild, peeling his shirt up his back and dragging it over his head. Then she was touching him, feeling his nipples, his arms, his ribs. Gabe moaned, running his hands over any part of her he could reach.

Calli urged his head back, grasping his jaw and kissing him heavily, her tongue slipping between his lips, slick and sliding.

"Make love with me, Gabriel." A heady plea, lush and sexy.

She felt wicked, in a darkened truck on the side of the road, her hunger for this man pushing her to take when he teased, demand when he hesitated. She brushed her breasts back and forth across his chest and he gripped her tighter and sank his finger inside her softness, stroking her wildly. She arched, bending back, and his mouth found her nipples again, working the tender tips into taut, sensitive buds. The only sound was heavy breathing and a soft sucking.

The heat of her sex warmed against his groin. His jeans felt like paper, nothing shielding the burning he had for her. His mouth moved over her skin, her stomach, her waist, but the confines of the cab wouldn't allow them freedom. Gabe wanted more and groped blindly for the passenger door handle. It sprang and he dragged her with him to the edge of the seat, opening the door wide. Calli's legs dangled over the side of the cushion as he backed out.

His boots touched the ground.

She spread her thighs and captured him between. She ducked her head and covered his flat nipple with her lush mouth, her hands roaming heatedly over his skin. He groaned like a tiger let loose, felt branded like a wild beast as her hands slid inside his jeans, over his hips to the lean curve of his buttocks. Gabe didn't think there was anything better than Calli touching him.

He kissed her hard, holding her tight, as if she might escape him, and tasted her throat, scraped his teeth over her mouth, her chin, down to her breasts, suckling one, then the other, before gliding his tongue down her stomach. He glanced up. She was watching him, her chest heaving with every breath, her hands running voraciously over his arms, his face. It did something strange to Gabe to know she would look at him like that. Eager, hungry, lovingly. She smiled like a cat and he lowered one knee to the ground.

Then he tasted her.

She cried out, the sound lost in the darkness of the desert and Gabriel drove deeply, scooping his hand beneath her buttocks and lifting her to the heat of his mouth. He felt her pulsing, her delicious squirming, heard her moans and whimpers. He lived in each sound, each movement, let them wrap around him, feed him. She was sweeter than wine, sweeter than her creations, and he devoured her pleasure.

Calli thought the world had opened up and drained her into the hot center. She couldn't catch her breath; he wouldn't let her. She jerked and flexed against his touch, her muscles tense, and then she was falling, bathed in fast heat and pulsing pleasure. He moaned and flicked his tongue and she shrieked his name. He chuckled darkly, dragging his mouth across her thigh, biting her flesh, tasting her lush body up to her mouth. Then she tasted herself on his lips.

"I want you," she panted. "Right now." She jerked open his jeans, peeling the fabric down and freeing him into her hand. Gabe clasped her roughly to him.

"Calli, I—"

"Yes, Gabriel," she insisted. "Don't deny us this." She stroked the tip of him against her softness, wetting him. He cursed softly and she felt his body tremble. "Inside me. I need to feel you. Please."

Gabe thought he'd lose any ounce of restraint right there. Then she kissed him again, her lips, her tongue, her body rocking against him was more temptation than any man could handle. He groped for the glove box, kissing her, sifting frantically through the debris of road maps and extra sunglasses for a condom. Luckily, he found one. She caught his hand, taking it from him, their breathing harsh, her eyes on him as she tore it open and rolled it down. The thought of being inside her was enough to spoil it for him, but he ground his teeth and his shoulders tensed as he waited for a fraction of the rushing desire to recede. He wasn't going to ruin this.

"You're sure about this?" He couldn't believe he was asking now.

"Oh yes."

"Not sore from riding?"

She flexed deliciously against him. "Do I look like I am?"

"Then wrap your legs around me." She did, and he lifted her enough to close the door, then pressed her back against the cold steel. The heat of her burned him and he shuddered, poised.

"Now, Gabriel, please."

In one thrust, he filled her deeply. She gasped his name. He trembled like a child, his lips whispering over her face.

And Gabe never felt so vulnerable than in that moment.

He withdrew and pushed, groaning weakly with every slow motion, and she sensed his restraint.

"Harder, Gabriel—" her fingers plowed through his hair "—I want all of you—" then dribbled down his chest to where they joined. "Don't hold anything back from me. Please." He drove into her, hard, and Calli laughed and matched him, met him, their bodies straining. The truck swayed with the force of their loving. He clutched her buttocks, rocking her in a heavy flowing motion, nothing subtle, nothing left to mystery. They wanted and they took. Calli was wild for Gabe, calling his name, raking her nails over his back, feeling where they meshed and molded. Hard lanced into soft, yielding to him, sheathing him lushly and Gabriel hungered for more.

She wrapped her legs tighter, her arms around his neck as he pushed and plunged into her, quick and hot and mindless. Her breath shuddered in his ear, her body racing to catch the elusive pleasure, then they caught it, his explosion wild and throbbing. His deep groan rasped in her ear as she joined him, heat and blood singing through her, masculine strength pulsing, feminine flesh gripping him, draining him. He called her name like a chant and never stopped until he could catch his breath.

He buried his face in the curve of her throat and clutched her tighter, unmoving for several moments. Gabe didn't want to go anywhere. He wanted to stay with her locked around him like a second skin, let her steal her way deeper into his heart and forget the world that moved and lived beyond this moment.

Her fingers played a pattern over his back, her teeth capturing his lobe, nipping him there.

He cupped her face in his broad palms and kissed her, a reverence he couldn't deny, a joy he'd never known. He smoothed his thumbs over her cheeks, searching her eyes in the dark.

"I hurt you, didn't I?"

"No," she cried in a whisper. "Of course not."

"God, Calli. That was…"

"Savage?" she offered with an innocent wide-eyed look.

He grinned crookedly. "Something like that." Gabe didn't understand what he was feeling. Ease? Contentment? He'd never felt quite like this after sex. And as he gazed into her wide blue eyes, even in the moonlight he knew it wasn't sex, wasn't anything that simple.

Calli smoothed a finger over his wrinkled brow. "What are you thinking?"

"That my rear's cold."

She smiled, but knew that wasn't it. She wasn't going to fill herself with recriminations and misgivings and told herself not to read anything into this than what it was; two people desiring each other and consenting.

He opened the cab door and set her on the seat, then eased from her body. Calli flopped bonelessly back onto the seat. Gabe turned away slightly and adjusted his clothing. It would scare her, he thought, if she knew he not only wanted her again, but was ready to do something about it.

When he turned back, she was half twisted on the seat, face-down, her sweet bottom in the air as she searched for her blouse.

"You teasing me again?" he murmured, smoothing his hand up over her buttocks.

"Oh, of course." She pushed back into his touch and tossed her bra over her shoulder, then glanced at him. He dragged it from his face. She laughed throatily as she sat up and slipped on her shirt, and Gabe couldn't help noticing her nipples pushing against the soft fabric. He caught her to him and bent, closing his lips over one plump bud, wetting the fabric.

She shuddered in his arms and sank her fingers into his hair. When he straightened, she had a glazed look in her eyes. He liked it. She reached behind her for his shirt and fitted it over his head, then when he pushed his arms into the sleeves she smoothed it over his chest. Gabe enjoyed every second of her touching him.

He gave her a sly look. "Where are your panties?"

"Check your pocket."

He did and pulled the yellow scrap out. She offered her foot. He shook his head. "They're mine." He stuffed them back where he'd found them.

In the moonlight, she blushed. "Adding it to a collection?"

"No!"

His reaction made her smile. "Good. Another first, I bet."

He eyed her, wondering if he should be pleased or insulted. She smiled like a cat with a mouthful of bird, and Gabe, having given up on trying to figure her out, climbed over her into the cab, then dropped behind the wheel with a groan. He started the engine, eased onto the road. She rubbed her arms and he pulled her close to his side.

"Now admit it," she said after they'd driven a mile, toying with the small loop in his lobe. "Wasn't that better than a cold shower?"

He glanced at her, a look she couldn't decipher in his pale eyes. "Calli," he said, his voice holding an odd regret. "Making love with you is better than breathing."

# Eleven

They stood in the living room, watching through the window as Bull drove away.

"He knows," she said, a light blush in her cheeks.

Her lips were swollen and she had red marks from his beard on her throat and the swells of her breasts, but he wasn't going to bring attention to that.

"What makes you say that," Gabe replied, hiding a smile, although his gaze lowered to her breasts, her nipples bare beneath the tank shirt and pushing against the fabric. She nudged him, blushing redder. He swept his arm around her waist, pressing his mouth to her temple as he murmured, "But the man would definitely have a heart attack if he knew you were completely naked beneath that skirt."

"Think so?" She tipped her head to look at him, speculative. "It did have a rather interesting effect on you, though."

"God, yes," he groaned, then pulled her flush against him, kissing her, stripping her, dragging her with him as he backstepped into her room.

"Why are we in here?" she said breathlessly as she peeled his

T-shirt off over his head. His anxiousness aroused her, his lips firm on her skin and his hands roaming frantically over her body.

"Something I've wanted since that first night in your hotel room."

She opened his jeans, sinking her hand inside, and he choked. She arched a brow; he look mischievous. "To talk nasty to me?" She stroked him heavily and a tremor racked his tall body.

"No, baby—" He fumbled in his back pocket, tearing open the foil pouch with his teeth. "To do it."

He lifted her up onto the dresser and pushed inside her, surging deeply, letting her feel every inch of him before Calli could catch her breath. Then he withdrew and pushed, slowly. She pounded his shoulders, scraped her teeth over his jaw, and he refused to move any faster, loving her squirming, her begging, her pleas to end her torture. He wouldn't, anchoring her hips and moving with a lazy erotic cadence, watching her eyes flare, her lips part with each ragged breath, feeling her fingertips dig into his shoulders as her body peaked with pleasure.

Gabe held her tightly in his arms, absorbing her rush of desire, her climax spiraling from her and into him. He kissed her and kissed, lush and thick, and before the heat faded he carried her to the shower, drenching her with tepid water and hot kisses. He made love to her again. *Made love to her.* She was breathless and panting against him and he swore if he could, he would spend all day right there under the water, letting her soap him and touch him. Ah, yes, her touching him was the best.

Naked, he took her back to the house, into his room and Calli hardly gave the surprisingly richly appointed room a glance. But he had a magnificent sleigh bed and they sank onto the mattress, a wild tangle of arms and legs as they slept.

Hours later, Gabe stirred and reached for the body he wanted pressed against him and found her gone. Immediately he sat up and looked around, then pulled on his jeans. His heart skipped with apprehension and for a moment he thought she might have left. Then he dismissed it. Calli wasn't a chicken. She would tell him if she was regretting sharing his bed, his life. She, above all else, was honest.

*And you're not,* a voice pestered. Gabe shoved the thought to the recesses of his mind, unwilling to spoil the past hours. He would deal with it when he had to and not before. He heard noise outside and after checking her room, he removed his gun from his desk drawer and left the house. Kerosene lights lit the porch and he found her. He set the gun aside. She looked up as he approached.

"Hi."

"Come back to bed, baby," he growled in a voice still rough from sleep as he slid his arms around her waist. She wore a thick, green terry robe and something deliciously enticing hinted beneath. He wanted to see it.

Calli tilted her head as his mouth found the curve of her throat.

"Cooking? At this hour?" Gabe said as she slid a plate in front of him.

"My latest creation. Sort of a birthday celebration."

He caught her chin and looked her in the eye. "Is it your birthday?"

"No, and I figured you didn't know when yours was, either, so today it is."

He smiled and stared down at the dessert. In the middle of the night she thought of this, in the middle of the night she gave him something he never had. A birthday. Gabe lifted his gaze to hers.

"Gabe?" she said, frowning softly.

"Thanks, Cal." He clutched her, his arms so tight she fought to breathe, but Calli let him. She'd seen the shock and pleasure in his eyes, the wonder. My Lord, that so little could make this man this happy, she thought, stroking his back. After a long moment he looked at her, his eyes suspiciously bright. "Can I eat it?"

She held up a fork and he took the dish and moved to a chair. In the cool night, he drew her onto his lap and then ate the dessert of brandied peaches laced with thick cream and toasted coconut. There was a light cake or something beneath it. It amazed him that she could create this so quickly.

"Got a name for it?" he said around a mouthful.

She looked at him for a second, then smiled. "Gabriel's Delight."

"I can think of something that would delight Gabriel," he

growled, using the fork to pull her robe aside. Calli's breath quickened.

He spread her robe and forked a gooey warm slice of peach, letting the heavy cream drip onto her breast. He ate the peach, then bent to drag his tongue over the lush swell of her breast.

Calli shivered in anticipation as he lowered his head, then gasped shortly as his lips closed over her nipple. He laved at the lacy green fabric, then hooked his finger inside the cup and dragged it down. He blew on her nipple and it puckered for him before he drew it heavily into the heat of his mouth. He suckled and stroked till she was breathless and slick and squirming. Then he slowly sat back and as casually as he could, finished off the dessert.

"Excellent, Cal. Four stars as usual."

His bland expression sent up a challenge. "Glad you like it," she managed, leaving his lap. "I was inspired." She took the empty plate and slid it into the tub. "Though Lord knows by what."

A dark chuckle rumbled in the night, but Calli refused to look at him. She closed her robe and listened as he stood and walked toward her. She wanted him. It was absolutely decadent the way she craved this man. There was something much more precious and greedy in receiving gentleness from Gabriel, because he thought himself incapable of giving it. Calli cherished every touch, every sliver of himself he gave to only her and he stole a piece of her soul every time his fingers whispered over her skin, his lips covered hers, his rough voice spoke. In a lifetime, she would never have enough of him.

Suddenly she felt his presence, the heat of him behind her.

"You really think that's going to get me mad?"

"No, I never intended it to." She didn't look at him.

"If you want me to...make love to you, I will."

"No, thank you very much."

Gabe grinned at her straight back. Always polite. Who'd have thought she was a clawing wildcat when he was inside her?

"You sure?" he said near her ear and thought she flinched.

"Yes...quite."

"Positive?" He pulled her robe open and down her shoulders, letting it fall to the floor.

"Only fools are positive," she whispered as his hands rode up her arms to unclasp her bra. He drew it aside, exposing her to the chilling night air. He adored the sound of her breath, fast and ragged, that she stood still, ignoring him, yet letting him do what he pleased. Trust, he thought, and hesitated briefly before he hooked the strip of fabric curling across her hip and lowered to the floor as he eased the panties down, kissing the curve of her spine, the rise of her buttocks.

"I want to make love to you here, outside," he said against the back of her thigh. "On the table, before God and anyone."

He stood slowly, his body brushing hers and from his vantage point he noticed her tight firm breasts were prickled with cold. He covered the lush mounds with his palms and nuzzled her neck. "But it's too cold."

She closed her hands over his. "Then take me inside, bad boy, and warm me." He swept her into his arms and strode inside. And he did just that.

At dawn, Gabe woke with her beside him, her body cocooned to his chest and thighs. He let his hands ride over her bountiful shape, cupping one plump breast, and she snuggled closer. "Time to get up," he whispered.

She moaned, then rolled over, facing him. "Mmm, make the world go away, Gabriel," she said sleepily, and dropped little pecks to his chest. "I know you can do it." She searched under the sheets and found him, hard and warm. "Oh, Gabriel," she breathed.

Gabe groaned and pushed her onto her back. She chuckled throatily, a rich, generous sound as she spread her thighs, taunting him with her sleep-rumpled warmth. "Think we can find another condom in this place?"

He gasped for air as she stroked him and struggled to reach the nightstand. He fumbled frantically, then showered her with a handful.

"Sure of yourself, or do enough women parade through—"

He covered her mouth with his, stopping her teasing. "I haven't been with a woman in two years," he said against her lips. "And I've never made love to one." A pause and then a scarcely whispered, "Till you," before he smothered her with a heavy kiss.

Calli's throat grew tight and her eyes misted. Gabe didn't give anything about himself easily. He was too proud to admit he'd no family, no love in his life, and she tried to tell herself she was reading too much into his confession. Wasn't she? Regardless, her heart broke open and hope flooded in.

When he pulled back, his gaze sharpened on her and his brows drew tight.

Avoiding the intensity of his gaze, she looked down at the foiled squares littering her bare chest. "Probably should check the expiration dates then, huh?"

They searched the pile, tossing some onto the floor, and when she found one, it was on him and he was inside her. He surged forward, one hand braced on the curving headboard, the other beneath her hips, bringing her to him, and Gabriel died a little inside as he watched passion enfold her body, wrap around him and hide him in a little place in her heart. This was all he would have of Calli, he knew. He knew he wasn't good enough for a lifetime, knew he was good enough only here.

Geyser and Deek were already hard at work when Bull arrived later that morning. He immediately sought out Calli and handed her a heavy white-and-blue envelope. Gabe noticed she merely glanced at the contents and tossed it onto the table. Later Bull confessed that it was the courier package of her traveler's checks he'd picked up at the post office. It gave Gabe an uneasy feeling. She had money and no real reason to stay now. His gaze went to her car, her trunk, and he wondered if he would ever have the chance to search it. Closing his eyes, he dismissed the idea. If she was going to stay, he wasn't going to jeopardize it yet. He lifted his gaze to where she stood under the porch, dressed in red shorts and a white T-shirt.

She'd been creating all sorts of high-calorie, high-fat desserts since just after breakfast. And Gabe was on sugar overload by lunchtime. Every time she made something new, she insisted Gabe be her taster. He was going to be ill, he thought, just pleasing her, his last occasion to sample mocha crème parfaits with shaved chocolate and a powder of almonds. Gabe admitted the desserts were beyond good, but the presentation was what made them Calli's. And Excalibur millions. She created one she called Guinevere's Tears. It was dark chocolate-cherry mousse in the shape of a knight's shield, covered smoothly in chilled white chocolate, intricately detailed with red crystal-like tears bleeding from the center. Romantic, Gabriel thought, lifting his gaze to hers. No, he corrected. Calli.

"I'll save these for after dinner." She slid the tray into the fridge.

Geyser and Deek groaned. "Just one taste, Miss Calli?"

She shook her head and took the spoon Geyser was licking like a child, then gently pushed him toward the barn. "Go work off that sugar, and I'll think about raising your cholesterol later," she said. The boys smiled and raced off.

Gabe watched them go, then looked at her. "They like you."

"They idolize you."

He scoffed. "Yeah, right." He stood and finished off a glass of tea.

"Don't you see it?" She nudged him and he turned to look. "They wouldn't work that hard for just anyone, Gabe. It's because you can relate to them, you understand them. Even if you never told them anything about yourself. They feel it."

"Feel what?"

"That you truly care about keeping them out of trouble and giving them a chance. You respect them."

He stared at the boys who looked more like men for their abused childhood. It was tough being sixteen and alone, locked in juvenile hall, Gabe thought, remembering when Daniel had given him a chance.

"I suppose."

Calli sighed. Would he never believe in himself? "Go work off that sugar, Griffin, before you get fat." Her gaze lingered over his washboard stomach and thickly muscled chest. It would be just like him to be able to eat nonstop and never gain an ounce, she thought peevishly.

"I can think of a better way to burn some calories," he offered, snagging her as she passed with a stack of dishes. He buried his face in her soft, scented neck and wanted more. A whistle cut the air and Gabe looked up. Geyser and Deek were laughing to themselves.

"See," she said, "they're really still just children."

She admired that Gabe took a chance on them like the man who had taken a chance on him. And Calli wondered if he'd give the same to her. As he brushed his mouth across hers and murmured a sexy, "See ya later, baby," in that to-die-for, knee-weakening voice, Calli knew she was in love with him, knew it from the first moment he'd confessed something private to her in her hotel room. Oh, it had taken her a while to fall, but the tumble started then. He was quiet and private and still harbored secrets. But they didn't matter to her. She loved him. And she would never tell him. He would clam up and push her out. Commitment wasn't a strong point with him or he wouldn't still be single. Or so alone.

*Like you?* her conscience pestered. Calli quickly cleaned up the mess, scribbled the recipe on a scrap of paper and stuffed it into her back pocket. She would enter it in her journal later. Now she wanted to be more than the ranch cook.

The past two weeks were the happiest Gabe had ever been in his life. Beyond the ranch there was reality, yet he indulged in having Calli living with him. He'd made love to her every night, sometimes fast and quick, leaving them breathless and laughing, and more often, slow and leisurely in his bed, indulging in the taste and feel of each other. She'd taught him to play chess and he'd taught her how to ride like a pro. He'd feasted on the finest food in his life and she'd feasted on him, giving herself without question, trusting him completely. He was weak at the sight of her and grew hard when she did something as simple as smile at him. They'd fallen into a routine that Gabe adored, lying on the couch together after everyone had left, where they would talk or read. Days ago she'd asked him to read aloud to her, insisting he had a voice meant for it. In the middle of a story, he'd told her that he'd only learned when he was twelve or thirteen, confessing that he didn't have much of an education. With the gentleness that was Calli, she'd called him a liar and said he was far more educated in what truly mattered.

She was on the sofa now, her back braced on the arm, her legs stretched out. Her journal was on her lap, her hand writing furiously. The huge day planner was stuffed with scraps of paper, sticky notes, paper napkins with writing on them. Gabe tried not to even look at it. The damn thing was like a pariah seeking him out. He had the irresistible urge to burn it.

Gabriel dropped onto the cushion and pulled her feet onto his lap. She crossed a *t* and looked up, her face brightening. "Hi."

She leaned out for a kiss and he gave it, then nodded to the journal. "Making notes?"

She looked down. "Yeah, came up with three more recipes. At least Daniel will be pleased."

"Will he?" Did he sound as casual as he hoped?

"Lord, yes. I couldn't create anything exceptional enough for the winter line a couple of weeks ago. Which is why I went on a vacation. Or rather, Daniel insisted I take one." She smiled mischievously. "I just didn't go where he wanted."

"No, you went looking for danger."

*No,* she thought, *I went looking for you.*

"Yeah," she purred, "and look what I found." She wiggled her toes in his side. He laughed and she was about to tickle him again when he grabbed her feet and rubbed the soles.

She moaned. "Hail Mary, that feels good."

He let his hand ride up and down her leg. "You worked hard today."

She smiled. She'd spread hay, shoveled dung, and even had the nerve to get on a horse again and ride the fields. Gabe grew his own feed, used water from the stream, and was nearly self-sufficient. "Two weeks ago you would have told me I was in the way."

"Maybe."

She nudged him in the stomach with her foot and he made a show of folding over. "You know you would have."

He turned toward her, like a panther stalking a mouse, and crawled on top of her, setting his weight gently over hers. She worked the journal from between them and set it on the floor.

"I'm beat." He laid his head on her chest and she sifted her fingers through his dark hair. It was a long moment before he asked, "Why did you do it, Cal?" He slid his arms around her, hugging her tightly. "You could have taken a nap or something."

"Thank you for reminding me that I am a poor ranch hand," she muttered dryly, and he looked up.

"I didn't mean—"

She pressed her fingers to his lips. "I know." She smiled tenderly, tracing the lines in his face with her fingertip. "I wanted to be a part of it. I never felt that way about much before, not that I didn't want to." She shrugged. "And I wanted—" she met his gaze "—to be with you."

"Good."

Her brows rose. "Really?"

"Saved me from thinking of an excuse to come hunt you down."

His admittance touched her deeply. "Now why would you do that?"

He inched up and whispered in her ear, whispered erotic words of what he wanted to do to her, how he would, and she felt a tingling heat skate up and down her body. "Is that possible?" she asked, nudging him so she could taste his mouth.

"Let me show you."

And boy, did he.

Bull came around the back of the barn and handed him the cellular phone. Gabe instantly looked for Calli. She was in the yard, teaching Geyser and Deek some karate, and a smile unwillingly shaped his lips. A black belt. No wonder she could dump him on his butt so easily. He looked back at Bull and moved out of sight.

"What?"

"Gabe? Daniel."

"I figured that."

"Not going well, huh?"

The concern in Daniel's voice hit Gabe like a mallet. Yes, he thought it was going great. He wanted Calli to stay and he'd broken a personal code by not following through with what he'd promised Daniel.

God, he didn't want to do this.

"Tell me you have everything cleared up, Daniel."

"No."

Gabe cursed, shoving his fingers through his hair, then mashing them over his face.

"But almost," Daniel added. "Did you get it back?"

"No."

"For heaven's sake, Gabe, what's the holdup?"

Gabe didn't respond, but his sigh was audible.

"Oh, God," came through the phone.

"Guess I don't need to explain then, huh?"

"I swear, Gabe!" There was a soft hiss through the phone and Gabe knew Daniel was trying to control his temper. "Just get it tonight and send her home, dammit." The line went dead and Gabe knew Daniel was angry. He collapsed the phone and tossed it in the tack room. Then with a burst of fury, he kicked the door shut.

Bull came around the corner, scowling. "Got a problem, son?"

Gabe stared at the hay-strewn floor, rubbing the back of his neck, his tall body a dark silhouette against the sun streaming through the open doors. "No. I'm fine." But he wasn't. He was so twisted inside he didn't know what to do. He owed Daniel, that was a given. But to repay by betraying Calli?

He could just go to her, tell her everything, then let her rant and rave and hope she would forgive him. Gabe couldn't risk it. He had to get the memo without her knowledge, and then nothing would happen. She would stay and he could go on loving her—

His head jerked up, his eyes wide. He stared at the barren wood wall.

He loved her.

Hell, he'd never loved a woman before, so how the hell did he know what he was feeling? All he knew was that when she walked into a room he was happy, when she smiled at him and touched him, he could almost cry from the sweetness of it. He wanted Calli in his life forever and he found himself late at night, watching her sleep in his arms, imagining a life with her, a family maybe. A damn dream, Griffin, a dream.

Things are different beyond this ranch. She would go back and remember him as if he were a summer fling when she was a teenager. He wasn't good enough for a lifetime with Calli. He couldn't trust his feelings for her. And he couldn't tell her. She would think he meant marriage and kids with a man like him. God, that was a laugh. He might be a decent lover in her eyes, but husband material? No way.

And what did he have to offer her. Debts? How could he ask her to stay? She was educated and rich, with a career that made her the toast of the culinary world. Hell, he'd picked up a copy of *Bon Appétit* while they were in the grocery store last week, out of sheer curiosity, and was stunned to see an article about her. It brought home just how different they were, again. Even though she dismissed it to hype for the winter line, Gabe wasn't fooled. She wouldn't be happy at the ranch, not for long.

All through dinner, he racked his brain for a solution. He didn't want to hurt her and felt he could get this matter out of the way without her knowing. It was deceiving, he knew, but what was that compared to lying to her flat-out? Or losing her? He remained in the barn shoeing a horse, avoiding her and facing his crime.

After supper she caught his arm, her blue eyes searching his, and Gabe clasped her roughly to him and kissed her in front of the ranch hands. And then he kissed her some more before he went back to work. It wasn't until the boys came to say goodbye that he realized it was nearly sundown. Bull's truck followed the van down the long dark road.

He left the barn and stopped short when she was nowhere in sight. Walking to the house, he found it empty, and he searched. He heard the splash of water and rapped on the bathroom door.

"Come in."

Gabe's breath caught. She was in a sea of bubbles, her head and shoulders exposed and she sank back and draped her arms over the edge of the old claw-footed tub.

"Want to join me?" She flicked water at him and he offered a small smile.

"Got to make a town run."

She frowned.

"Some supplies."

She started to get out of the tub.

"No, you stay, enjoy that." He gestured to the bubbles. "It will only take me an hour at the most. I'm going to lock you in. Okay?"

She nodded, trying not to frown. "Come here." He stepped inside, shutting out the draft, and knelt beside the tub. "What's bothering you?"

"Nothing, baby, just tired."

She didn't believe him, even though he had four more horses to care for than a week ago. She cupped his jaw, tipping his face to hers and gazing into his eyes. She saw defeat there, regret and maybe a little anger. What had happened? she wondered. She adored this man but he was going to have to learn to share more. And it would start with her.

"There is something I've been meaning to tell you."

Me too, he thought, his heart squeezing in his chest. He covered her hand pressed to his cheek.

"I love you, Gabriel."

He closed his eyes, his fingers flexing over hers. "Cal—"

"No. Don't say anything. I love you. That's all."

*That's all? Is that enough?* a voice sounded in his brain like a thunderclap. He learned over and kissed her, a brief brush of his lips that shattered her heart. Without a glance, he stood and left, closing the door behind him. Calli sank into the bubbles and tried not to cry. He didn't love her back.

Beyond the door, Gabe sagged against the wood. His eyes burned and he shut them tightly. *I love you, Gabriel.* He never thought anyone would say those words to him. Ever. He wanted to grab her up and run for the hills where no one could find them, nothing could harm them. He almost wished she'd never said those words. It made it harder to do what he'd promised. He swore he was out of the private investigating business after this.

He pushed away from the door and strode across the room to where her journal lay spread on the coffee table. He searched, found the memo tucked in the back, with an itinerary of a Mexican tour she'd never taken. He replaced everything as it was, then stuffed it in his back pocket. He wasn't going to send it to Daniel, he was going to burn it.

Calli gave up trying to read the book and tossed it onto the coffee table. He'd been gone over an hour. She was worried. Without the distraction of a television, she had little beyond her own imagination to comfort her. She rewrapped her robe and reached for her journal. Propping it on the arm, she scanned her notes by candlelight, then picked up her pen. She wrote hard and suddenly ran out of ink. Cursing under her breath, she stood, took the candle and walked to his desk, hunting for a pen. It was awkward, trying to search with a candlestick in her hand. She opened the top right drawer and saw his gun, nudged it out of the way as if it were a snake, then dug deeper. Nothing. How could that man function without a pen? Sitting down, she riffled the center drawer and was about to close it and give up when something caught her attention.

Excalibur stationery.

Her hand trembled as she lifted the sheet out. Her heart sank to her stomach. Tears filled her eyes. It was addressed to Gabriel Griffin, Private Investigator, from Daniel O'Hara. And it was about her.

# Twelve

The door rattled and she looked up as he stepped inside.

His gaze went immediately to her. Then to the paper in her hand, the shadow of the gold-embossed letterhead reflecting clear in the candlelight.

Gabriel's heart clenched painfully as he brought his gaze to hers. The look in her eyes was like a switchblade slicing his throat. Agonizing. Hopeless.

She stood slowly. "You're a private investigator." Her tone was dead. Flat.

"Yes." He shrugged uneasily. "Sometimes."

"Apparently a very good one," she said, tossing the paper onto the desk, her usual soft voice gone bitter with anger. "I thought your name was familiar, but I couldn't remember where I'd seen it." Her hand trembled as she brushed her hair back from her face. "Now I do." He really had been talking with Daniel that day in her hotel room.

"I couldn't tell you, Cal. Client confidentiality."

"How convenient for you." Her voice wavered and she swallowed repeatedly.

Gabe said nothing, looking away. But he could feel her hurt with every indrawn breath and it surrounded him, bludgeoning a hard fist against his heart.

"You were hired to follow me, to protect me from what? Who?"

He brought his gaze to hers. "Murdock and anyone who wants your work for Excalibur."

"For a winter line I hadn't even created?" She snapped her hand toward the letter. "If he wanted the damn recipes enough to hurt me, trash my room, let loose your colt, I would have gladly given them to him!" she stormed as she moved around the desk, her eyes sharp with anger. "They don't mean that much to me, Gabe, and I can always create more."

He held her gaze, searching for the woman he'd held only hours ago. "He wanted to hurt you, Cal."

She scoffed and he could tell she was fighting tears. "He hurt *you*. You had more to lose than me and a few recipes."

Losing her was worse than dying and he was watching it happen. "Calli, I didn't want you to find out like this." He stepped closer.

She retreated. "Well, I did. When were you going to tell me? After you made love to me for the hundredth time?"

"There never was a good time."

"Then why, Gabriel?" Her voice fractured, broke over his name.

His client confidentiality in tatters, he said, "Daniel asked me to get a memo you had."

Daniel had known all along where she was. Damn them. "The one about Rodrigez?" He scowled. "I've seen it. Only this morning." She bent and riffled through the thick planner. Her hand stilled when she realized it wasn't there. Slowly she straightened, her shoulders drooping. "You went through my things," came with utter despair. She lifted her gaze to his, raking him and finding him short of her expectations. "All you had to do was ask, Gabe." Fat tears filled her eyes, rolling down her cheeks. Gabe withered inside with each one. "You must think I'm really stupid."

"No! Come on, Cal—"

She put up her hand to stop the explanation she didn't want to hear. "Daniel is wrong and he'll find out soon enough. But you could have been honest."

His spine stiffened, his expression unreadable. "I had a job to do."

"And I trusted you!" she cried, clutching her robe, nearly folding over with her pain. "I trusted you, Gabriel. How could you do this to me? For a few dollars? Were you well compensated for the *duty* of kissing me, touching me, *making love to me?*" came a tortured sob.

Gabe's expression crumbled. "Baby, you have to know that isn't true." He plowed his fingers through his hair, his arms already aching to hold her. "God, I wished Daniel had never asked. But I owed him."

"And what did you owe me? I loved you! But you couldn't be honest with me. You didn't care about me. I was just a case to you."

"After all this—" he spread his arms "—is that what you think?"

"Tell me otherwise."

He stared at her, through her. The silence stretched. And Gabe was suddenly mortally terrified. Terrified of her leaving him and terrified of her staying; of confessing his heart and having it crushed. But she made him weak with longing for dreams he'd no right to seek, for an equal share of a relationship. He couldn't give her back what she needed, deserved, not in a lifetime. And the look in her eyes told him the respect she had for him was now burned to ashes.

Her next words were laced with such stinging agony, Gabe knew there was no repairing the damage he'd done.

"I see. Damn, I feel like a whore." His gaze shot to hers. "And you've shown me there really is no one here but *Angel.*"

She left the room, her hand over her mouth. But he heard her sobs. He could take anything but her tears, and every muffled whimper, every choke, tore through him, ripping and shredding what was left of his composure. His insides twisted, an unfamiliar rock filling his throat.

He hadn't moved when she came out of the room, dressed and

packed. She grabbed up her journal and stuffed it into her bag, then headed to the door. His fist clenched with the urge to grab her and beg her to stay.

Calli stilled on the threshold, casting a glance back over her shoulder. She held his gaze, silently pleading.

*Stop me. Tell me you love me and give me a chance to forgive you.*

But he didn't want forgiveness, she knew. It would be his punishment.

And her penance for loving him.

He stood motionless, even after he heard her car speed away.

Numbly, Gabriel stared at the room, his gaze drawn to a platter in the center of the dining table a few feet away. Carefully presented was a single shield of a fallen knight, bleeding his love's bitter tears. And a note, written before his crime. The simple words gouged his heart. *I will always love you, bad boy.*

Calli moved around the massive test kitchen with quick efficiency, snapping orders, correcting mistakes. Her apprentices were shell-shocked and when she accidentally knocked a metal bowl to the floor, they cowered. She sighed and bent to clean up the mess, peaches and cream sliding over her hands. The scent of it brought back unbearable pain with the force of a blow. Gabriel, his pale eyes and dark presence, his possessive kisses, the way he looked when he made love to her, the way he smiled.

And the way he'd let her walk out of his life. She choked back a sob and quickly cleaned up the mess.

"Calli?" Rodrigez whispered, bending to help. His shirtsleeves were rolled back, exposing a tattoo and her heart shattered again. Two weeks and she was still so numb. Nothing gave her any satisfaction. The harder she fought to keep Gabe out of her mind, the bigger he was, invading her work, her dreams, a silent phantom in her bed.

*He doesn't love you. He let you go.*

Calli felt like discarded baggage, used and pushed aside when the bubble burst. Her hands shook. Her mind wouldn't rest, her heart aching for a man who didn't want her beyond his bed. She knew he wasn't the commitment type and she was an utter fool to think she could change that. She felt wasted and barren inside. She could forgive that he'd taken pay to protect her, set up their meeting in the Nail, challenged her to get her out to his ranch. She even reasoned that because of some code of honor for a client, he couldn't reveal his circumstances. But what she couldn't take was that after all they'd shared, he could let her walk away without a second thought. Not even a cool, "It's been great, baby, see ya around." Not even a goodbye.

"I can't do this anymore," she whispered brokenly. She stood and headed to her offices, stripping off her white coat and tall hat.

"I won't accept it." Daniel sagged back in the big leather desk chair and tossed her resignation back at her.

"Then don't. I don't care."

She didn't care about much anymore, he thought sadly. Her energy was gone, her eyes lacked sparkle, her smiles rare and forced. This was the first time she'd spoken to him in two weeks and beyond losing his executive chef, he was losing a dear friend.

"Calli, honey, I'm sorry you got caught in the middle of this, but—"

She put up her hand, halting yet another explanation. "Daniel. I left for more reasons than lack of creativity. I hid out, which was a joke since you knew where I was, but I went with Gabriel to avoid you and *them*." She flung a hand toward the test kitchens and the apprentice chefs she knew had an ear glued to the separating door. "I know you all care about me, but you treat me like a child. Hail Mary, I couldn't go on a vacation without you prying into my life! If you'd given me credit for having a brain, if you'd been honest, you wouldn't have spent your hard-earned cash on a baby-sitter!" She took a deep breath and calmed her temper, her eyes bright as she stared out the wide window behind his desk.

"He was your bodyguard."

Calli thought of what Gabe did to her body and it wasn't in the job description. "I can't work here anymore." She leveled a hard look at him. "I don't want to."

She spun on her heels and exited the room. Daniel gazed at

the empty doorway. This whole mess had backfired. Except for Murdock. He'd approached Rodrigez and they'd caught Murdock, leveling charges of corporate espionage. Daniel was forced to admit Calli was right. The young parolee hadn't betrayed them. He'd already gone to the head of systems security and told him to be on the lookout. And the instant she'd returned, Rodrigez had confided in Calli.

Daniel was losing her to God knew what company or restaurant and not because he'd sent Gabe after her. She wasn't happy at Excalibur anymore. Gabe did his job too well, he thought. What had gone on, Daniel didn't want to know. He knew Gabe well enough to come to a few conclusions. None of them pleasant. He never expected Calli to be affected by the man. He was hard as diamonds and just as sharp. But if she's hurting this bad, he wondered, what about Gabe? Daniel adored Calli and could hardly bear her pain. She could never hide her feelings very well, anyway. She was everything a man wanted in a daughter and when his wife learned she was leaving because of his interference, he was going to suffer more than Calli. Heck. It couldn't get any worse, Daniel thought, and reached for the phone, dialing.

"Yeah."

"Good, you sound rotten. I don't know what went on in New Mexico, Gabe, but you sure as hell made a mess."

Silence and then, "What went on was you interfering in my life again, Danny boy."

Daniel's lips twisted in a wry smile. "Maybe, but I'm paying. Believe me."

"So."

Daniel plowed his fingers through his neatly styled silver hair. "She's leaving."

"Always knew Calli was a smart woman."

Daniel heard the catch in his voice when he said her name. He wasn't over her.

"No, not just Excalibur. She's leaving the state."

Another moment of painful quiet, then, "Afraid your business will go down the tubes?"

Daniel ground his teeth and spoke from the heart. "Calli means more to me than you'll ever understand, Gabe. She's a good woman and you need to clean up this mess so she can get on with her life.''

''She'll be fine.''

Daniel wondered how this man could spend weeks with a woman like Calli and still be so cold. ''You know, Gabe,'' he said philosophically, ''I never knew you to walk away from a second chance.''

''There isn't one this time.''

Daniel swung the leather chair around and stared out the wide window. ''How are you going to know, man, if you don't ask?''

There was a hesitation and Daniel could hear his frustrated sigh. Then the line went dead.

Gabe laid the phone down and dug the heels of his palms into his eyes, his elbows braced on his knees. Her expression, the look of utter devastation in her eyes, burst through his mind. Again. A lump thickened in his throat. *Aw, baby,* he thought, *I didn't mean to hurt you like that.* She was leaving her job, her home and vanishing. *Can't keep screwing up your own life,* he thought, *now you're screwing with hers.* But Gabe couldn't do anything about it. She was gone. He was alone. And Daniel's implication that he could ask for a second chance was a pipe dream. He had killed what they'd shared by lying to her after they'd been intimate.

He pushed off the bench and marched across the dry yard.

''Turn it around,'' Gabe snapped, pointing to Geyser's head and the ball cap turned backward. ''You're not on the block here, homeboy.''

Geyser glared at him from beneath a shock of blond hair, shifting his cap around before hefting the rake again. He scraped it across the yard, gathering large stones. ''What you do to make her go, Gabe?''

Gabriel stopped short and cocked a look back over his shoulder. His pale gaze pierced and warned.

''Never mind,'' Geyser muttered, and kept to his job.

''Where are you going?'' Gabe demanded of Bull as he passed him.

"Someone's got to feed these kids." Bull eyed him. "You want to do it?"

"No." He couldn't go near the kitchen without being slaughtered with memories.

"Thought maybe some of her talent rubbed off on you. Her sweetness sure as hell didn't." Bull glared back at him and with a curse, Gabe turned away and headed to the barn, ordering Deek to follow. Deek looked at the others, apprehension in his eyes before he obeyed.

"Sweep out number two and three, break open another bale, then water the McKinny horses."

Gabe picked up a shovel and piled dung into a wheelbarrow.

"Want me to walk Guinevere?"

"No!" Gabe roared as he spun around. Deek reared back, instinctively bringing his arms up to block his head. The move penetrated the guilty fog and he realized what he was doing, to all of them. His shoulders sank. He threw down the shovel and raked a dirty, blistered hand through his hair. He was making *them* pay for the hurt only *he'd* caused.

"Go, take a break." He waved Deek off and the boy vanished in a hard run.

Gabe leaned his back against the wall and slowly sank to the ground. He was bone tired, the dull ache in his chest heightening his weariness. He couldn't remember the last time he'd taken even a couple hours off, but his ranch was finally showing a profit. He'd already turned down two boarders for lack of stalls and would have to build another barn soon. But all the repairs and horses to train weren't going to erase the unspeakable loss he felt with every heartbeat. Calli was gone, yet she was everywhere. He rubbed his eyes, the sting reminding him he hadn't slept. He couldn't. His bedroom came alive with her scent every night, the memory of her body fitting to his, her hands on him. Gabe closed his eyes tightly, trying to push a list of necessary work into his brain.

He failed. God, he couldn't even eat without thinking about her. Every time he walked toward the house, he saw her in the shade of the kitchen, smiling, cooking, offering him samples and he especially remembered the look in her eyes when she'd found something he liked. It made him feel the damage he'd done to her again and again, forging a sorrow so unfamiliar he thought he would go mad. He needed her to survive, he admitted finally.

God, Gabe thought, pinching the bridge of his nose and blinking. He loved her so much it hurt to breathe.

Calli didn't bother to turn on the lights and tossed her keys on the credenza, kicking off her shoes as she moved to the sofa. She dropped into the soft cushions and put her feet up, leaning her head back and closing her eyes. Her apartment was quiet, painfully lonely. She supposed she ought to start packing, but lacked the motivation. Instead, she let her mind wander.

Mentally she ticked off chores to do, but her thoughts came back to Gabe. Always Gabriel. His face, his eyes. And always with a dull, hard throb in her chest. Lord, she missed him. Everything felt worthless and empty without him in her life and as she'd done every night since she'd left him, she argued with herself. She should have demanded reasons, pushed him to explain. But he hadn't offered them; he wouldn't tell you how he felt. The painful reality was that she'd gambled on the wrong kind of man and lost. She'd loved him, still loved him, even more than the moment he let her walk away.

"Hey, baby."

Her eyes flashed open. Her heart slammed against the wall of her chest, then sank like a stone. Gabriel. He was in her living room, his shoulder braced on the tall window frame, one hand in the pocket of his black pleated slacks, the other catching a short tailored jacket slung over his shoulder. His white collarless shirt contrasted against his tanned skin even in the darkness of her apartment. For a long moment she simply looked, absorbing the headiness of being near him again. Moonlight spilled through the sheer curtains behind him, shadowing his face, yet Calli's heart clenched as his gaze dipped and climbed over her body. She could feel it, it was so intense.

"How did you— Never mind." She tilted her head. "Does this mean you've returned to your old profession?"

"No."

"Daniel called you, didn't he?"

"Yes."

"Damn him!" She lurched out of the couch. "Being paid well this time?"

"You really think that?"

He heard her sigh. "No, I don't know what to believe anymore." She moved behind the sofa, switching on a light. Hesitantly, she lifted her gaze and inhaled sharply. He looked tired and tortured. "What do you want?"

Gabe could hardly control his need to hold her. A lump formed in his throat, the same one when he imagined her, remembered how much he'd hurt her and how much it hurt to live without her. He steeled his courage and jumped without a parachute.

"You."

Calli's heart beat so fast it threatened her breathing. She was thrilled he was here. Thrilled he looked as bad as she felt, but he was going to have to work for her this time.

Across the room they stared.

"You had me."

"I know."

"You let me leave." Her voice wobbled and she swallowed.

"After lying, I didn't have the right to ask you to stay."

"And what makes you think you do now?"

Her bitterness turned him back and his shoulders sank. "Nothing, I guess." He pushed away from the window frame.

Calli's heart crashed and burned. "Don't you dare walk away, Gabriel Griffin." He stilled, waiting. Her voice was wounded as she said, "Why couldn't you trust me when I trusted you?"

His gaze sketched her upturned face. "I wanted to. You don't know how much." He shook his head, infinitely sad. "But I'm not good enough for that."

"Oh, but *I* was only good enough for you to *sleep with,* but not love, huh?"

Gabe paled. "You know that's not true." Couldn't she see that just looking at her was killing him?

"Damn you, Gabriel! I know no such thing! For God's sake, you took a piece of my heart every time you touched me!"

Gabe remembered every moment they'd spent together. He'd been reliving it since he let her walk out the door. Her laugh; the way stupid peaches and coconuts made her teary-eyed; how she fought back and threw onions at him.

She was in front of him, gazing into his eyes. "Why did you come all the way to Texas?"

"I missed you."

She scoffed. "Missed regular sex maybe." And she walked away.

"Dammit, Calli!" He grabbed her by the arms and pulled her back. "You know it isn't that way between us. We're more than that! You can feel it now. *I* can feel it in you." He let a breath out through clenched teeth. "We belong."

Belong. Calli had never felt that until she was with him, until she loved him. "Then tell me, Gabriel," she whispered. "Why are you here?"

"I need you, Cal."

She frowned. "Need?" She wrestled out of his touch. "I need food, Gabe. I need showers and antiperspirant."

"Well. *I* never needed *anyone!* Never." She didn't speak, waiting, watching. "Hell, before, I was okay with being alone. It was the best for me and everyone else. I didn't mind being cut off. I'd been alone so long, it was all I knew." He glanced briefly away, swallowing. "But now…" He hesitated and took a breath, meeting her gaze. "I'm not doing too well without you, baby." His tone deepened, rasped. "And it's not getting any better."

She held his gaze. He was struggling to tell her his feelings. She knew Gabriel. It was the biggest step in his life to admit he was vulnerable, that he needed someone else.

He held his jacket in front of him by the collar like a shy cowboy holds his hat. "Cal…I know I hurt you—"

"Yes, you did, very badly."

His expression crumbled into utter regret. "I'm sorry, baby."

"I believe you." His pale eyes softened and the emotion she saw made her heart skip an entire beat. "Why did you let me leave, Gabe? Why didn't you call?" She was still far enough away that he couldn't touch her. If he did, she would be lost.

"Guilt. I'd lost your respect. I saw it in your eyes. You'd been honest and trusting and I betrayed you."

"I realize you were keeping your promise to Daniel."

"Screw Daniel," he growled. "I might have owed him for not having me arrested and giving me a job—" Calli's eyes widened as she made the connection. "But I'd ruined the best thing in my life and I thought I could deal with it." He looked at the ceiling, briefly closing his eyes, his breath hissing out before he met her gaze. "You forgave the world, but I couldn't hope you'd ever find it in you to forgive me."

"I do."

His strong features tightened and Calli felt a sudden energy running through him and connecting to her. Still, he hesitated. "Why are you so terrified of loving me, Gabriel?"

"Because I'm not sure I know how!" came an anguished rasp. "You're so gentle and giving and, dammit, Calli, I can't be those things for you!"

"Oh, Gabriel," she whispered. "You *are* those things. I don't need you to be anything else but who you are. If I wanted more or different, I would have never let you touch me. And I would never have stayed so long." She moved closer, her lush body a whisper away from his. "You try too hard to be bad, you know. You *are* a good man." He shook his head, but she caught his face in her palms. "A good man held a newborn foal all night. A good man found me peaches and coconuts. A good man gave his last dollar to a vagrant." She slid her hands down to his chest, feeling the frantic beat of his heart against her palms. "A good man shares his heart without expecting anything in return."

"But I want something now," he whispered, dropping the jacket. "Bad." Gently, he put his hands on her waist. "I know I don't deserve—"

She covered his lips with two fingers. "You deserve whatever you truly want, Gabriel."

His lips shaped to her fingertips and as she slowly lowered her hand, Gabe took a risk and asked for his life. "A second chance. I want you, with me. I can't live without you."

Calli's vision blurred and her heart roared. "Why?"

He wet his lips. "I love you, Cal."

She inhaled. Her gaze explored his, recognizing the truth that had been there all along.

"I need to know—" he asked, fear in his eyes, "Do you still love me?"

He'd confessed and still laid his heart on the stone, a solitary man risking rejection over and over to be certain. "Yes. Oh, yes."

"I love you, Calli." Her eyes bloomed with tears and he sank his fingers into her hair, cupping the back of her neck and pulling her against him. "I love you," he whispered, reverent. "From the moment you bit me, I swear."

She laughed, gazing at him through watery eyes. "I'll have to remember that." She wound her arms around his neck and stood on her toes. "Kiss me, hurry."

He did, slowly, his strong arms wrapping around her, tight and protective. His kiss was heavy and soulful, pouring his love into her. Calli could feel the release in him. The shedding of old hurts and past pains. Neither of them would be lonely or alone again.

He pulled back and scattered kisses over her face, urging her head back. "God, I've missed you so much, baby, so damn much," he murmured against her throat.

Calli gripped his biceps. "Oh, Gabriel."

His hold tightened, his kisses feverish, insistent. "I love it when you say my name."

"I love you, Gabriel."

He lifted his head to look at her, then kissed her, quick and hot. "Say it again."

She smiled, teary-eyed. "I love you." She ran her hands down his shirt, hurriedly plucking buttons. "And I want to show you." She pushed the fabric off his shoulders.

Gabe grinned as she caressed his chest, his arms, her fingers loosening his buttons. "Dangerous words, woman."

"Don't I know it."

He chuckled, peeling off her jacket, then attacking her blouse. She gripped the band of his trousers, pulling him along as she back-stepped down a short hall toward her bedroom. They were all over each other, groping, teasing, arousing. Suddenly Gabe couldn't wait and pushed her back against the wall, grinding his body to hers as he kissed her relentlessly and tugged at her clothes, opened her blouse. He moaned against her lips as he filled his palms with her breasts. It's been too long, he thought.

She called out his name, whimpered at the familiar heat escalating through her body.

"There's a bed a few feet away," she panted, licking his lips as she yanked open his belt buckle. His eyes flared and she sent the zipper down. His breath caught and she slipped her hand inside.

He was naked beneath.

"Oooh, you're wicked."

He choked as her hand closed over him. "Learned it from you," he managed to growl.

Kissing her greedily, he dragged her into the bedroom, kicking off his shoes, shaking off his shirt, then immediately stripping off her blouse. Desire flamed out of control, a savage need to come together making them clumsy. Gabe toed off his socks even as he reached for her skirt, sending it to the floor. She unclasped her bra and Gabe hesitated, watching as she freed her breasts. Then he pulled her roughly into his arms, one hand making a wild ride over her back, her satin-covered buttocks, the other cupping her breasts, his thumb circling her nipple. It felt so good to touch her again, to feel her skin on his, her hands on him.

She pushed his trousers down over his hips, stroking his firm flesh. He groaned darkly and kicked them aside.

"Calli..." He kissed the corner of her mouth. "Baby..." He scraped his teeth over her jaw, then down to her breast. "I want to go slow but—" He sat on the edge of the bed, pulling her between his thighs as he claimed her delicate nipple with his mouth. Calli clutched his head, hers thrown back as he tasted and teased. He hooked his thumbs in her panties and pulled, his mouth exploring her skin, reacquainting himself with the taste of her.

"Gabriel," she moaned, and he fell back, taking her with him, pulling her beneath him. She opened. He reached for a condom. She shook her head and guided his body home.

Eyes locked, a silent message of trust and love passing between them. She brushed hair from his forehead, felt him tremble.

"I love you," he whispered brokenly. Then he sank deeply into her softness. His features tightened, his eyes slamming shut for a second. "Oh, sweet mercy, you feel good."

"Oh, Gabe, I missed you. I missed you so much," she cried into his mouth.

"Me, too, baby. Oh, me, too." He clutched her, moving gently, and Calli answered, her body cradling his, stroking him, loving him. Her breath spilled in a ragged shudder. His hands slid beneath her hips, urging her closer. The cadence was at first smooth and urgent, then thrashing and raw. Friction brought tight, twisting pleasure, love gave it meaning and permanence. They strained and hungered, fingers dug, bodies arched, fused as they rocketed toward a shattering rapture unlike any before. They hovered on a mist of pleasure, blue eyes holding pale liquid green, before they sank into the still-made bed.

Her breathing still quick, Calli showered him with kisses along his jaw, his shoulder. She licked the artwork on his bicep and would soon fulfill her fantasy of tasting every inch of him.

Gabe gazed down at her, his body shaking with bone-splintering tremors. He brushed his lips over hers, unhurried. She was his heartbeat, his lifeline. The sheer agony that came with even thinking of being without her was too much.

Calli touched his handsome face, smoothed her thumb over his lips. "I love you, Gabriel Griffin. I always will."

"Then take a risk with me, Calli." He pressed a kiss to her fingertips. "A big one."

"I think we just did."

Tender humor lit his features as his fingers combed her hair from her face. "A bigger one." His pale eyes probed.

"Gabe?"

His throat worked, his voice an emotion-thick growl. "Marry me, baby."

"Yes," she answered without hesitation. "Yes!"

He smiled, hugely, the corners of his eyes crinkling, his dimple showing. "Tonight."

She blinked.

"I've already wasted too much time. I want to get on with our life."

He'd finally let it go, she thought, the past and the pain of it. She was proud of him, loving him for his bravery. Then her expression was suddenly mischievous. "We could wake up Daniel to witness it?"

He offered a lopsided grin. "That could be dangerous."

"Well..." She shrugged naked shoulders. "They say only the good die young."

"No, baby, not this time." Never again, he thought, sinking into her soft embrace. They healed the wounded and lived forever. They went looking for Mr. Wrong and made them right.

# Epilogue

Gabe pushed open the door of Peaches and looked around the diner for his wife. Wife. Even after two years, he still couldn't believe she had married him.

The restaurant was packed and customers immediately called out a hello. Gabe smiled, answered, then strolled through the restaurant, its fifties' diner look, cleaner, sharper, more refined. Like her. He found her exactly as he'd left her this morning, hovering over a new menu, a stack of paperwork littering "their" table.

He stood back for a moment, watching, loving her more every time he saw her. If that were possible. Calli was more than his wife, she was his best friend. His partner. Gabe knew she'd been right all along, that he'd kept himself from people because he was afraid of being hurt, like when he was a kid. And hurting them back because he didn't know what real love was. But not anymore. She'd taught him how easy it was to accept, let go and then begin again. She'd taught him how easy it was to love and forgive. Every morning with her was a fresh start. Though he'd never had much faith in God, Gabe believed in Him now. No one could have a woman like her walk into his life and redefine it by just plain dumb luck.

"You're staring again."

He blinked and gave her a lopsided grin. "Lot of good stuff to stare at, baby."

Calli smiled, loving the goose bumps running over her skin every time he spoke to her like that, a hunger in his voice only she could recognize. Instead of sliding into the opposite seat, he sat down next to her. She propped her elbow on the table, her chin in her palm, and gazed into his eyes. Eyes so full of emotion she wondered how he could have hidden it away all those years.

"Your side not warm enough or something?" She inclined her head ever so slightly to the other seat, yet her eyes never left his.

"Like I said, good stuff's on this side." Under a tablecloth so white it glared, his hand slid up her thigh.

"Gabriel," she warned, yet her lips twitched with a smile.

"Yeah?"

"You're being wicked again."

"And you like it."

She leaned close, her right hand driving between his thighs and finding his hardness. "Oh, my, and so do you."

He inhaled deeply, his warm gaze raking her. "This time *everyone* is watching us."

"What a shame," she said as she teased him mercilessly for a few more minutes.

They turned to talk about the diner, that Daniel was pestering them to come visit, Bull had a new girlfriend, and that if Deek couldn't get a grant for college, they'd agreed to help out.

"When are you coming home?" Impatience laced his tone.

"Rodrigez is closing up tonight. So I'll be early. Give me a lift after you do the grocery shopping?"

He took the list she offered. "I'm gonna do more than give you a lift, baby."

She smiled seductively. "Oooh, threats! I like it."

He kissed her, long and hard, wrapping his arm around her waist and pulling her against him. "I love you, Cal. See you in a couple hours."

He slid from the seat, offering his hand and as she'd done since she bought the restaurant, she walked him to the front station by the door. He brushed his mouth over hers and squeezed her once, then reached for the handle.

"Oh, by the way," he said over his shoulder. "Guinevere is pregnant."

Something sparkled in her eyes just then. "Good," she called softly. "So am I." He started to open the door, then froze. He stared at the glass for a moment, then whipped around, his gaze wide and pinning.

He didn't have to ask if he heard right. Her smile was blinding enough.

He moved slowly toward her, his eyes never leaving hers, and he gathered her in his arms, covering her mouth with his. His hands fisted in her clothes, drove her hard against him, love and sweet passion melting through her into him.

Gabe kept kissing her, backing her into the alcove leading to her real office.

"Oh, God." In the darkened corner, he smoothed her hair back with both hands. "A baby." His throat bobbed, his gaze rapidly skimming her beautiful face. "Ours! I almost can't believe it."

She took his hand and pressed it to her hardness in her abdomen. "By Christmas you will."

He choked, his eyes unusually bright, his heart pounding in his chest, and swore if he wasn't ten feet from a restaurantful of people, he would sob like a two-year-old.

He pressed his forehead to hers, struggling for calm. "I adore you, do you know that?"

She nodded, sifting her fingers through his hair at his nape, too moved by his expression to speak.

"I never imagined anyone had a right to be this happy."

She touched the lines of his jaw, his cheek, feeling the shape of his lips. "We do, my love, we really do."

He tipped his head back, his tall body shuddering. "I believe it, baby."

"Sometimes, Gabriel Griffin—" She pressed a delicate kiss to his trembling lips and said, "You really are *such* a marshmallow. God help you if we have a girl."

He laughed softly, his eyes crinkling, and he slid his arms

around her. For a long time he simply held her, feeling their heartbeats match and mate. He'd only had two second chances in his life. One gave him a purpose, the other brought him out of pure hell and was still pulling him sweetly into heaven.

And he was loving every minute of the ride.

\* \* \* \* \*

# Return to the Towers!

In March
*New York Times* bestselling author

# NORA ROBERTS

brings us to the Calhouns' fabulous
Maine coast mansion and reveals the
tragic secrets hidden there for generations.

For all his degrees, Professor Max Quartermain has a
lot to learn about love—and luscious Lilah Calhoun is
just the woman to teach him. Ex-cop Holt Bradford is
as prickly as a thornbush—until Suzanna Calhoun's
special touch makes love blossom in his heart.
And all of them are caught in the race to solve
the generations-old mystery of a priceless
lost necklace...and a timeless love.

# *Lilah and Suzanna*
## THE
## Calhoun Women

### A special 2-in-1 edition containing
**FOR THE LOVE OF LILAH and
SUZANNA'S SURRENDER**

Available at your favorite retail outlet.

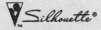

Silhouette®

# Take 4 bestselling love stories FREE

## Plus get a FREE surprise gift!

**ALICIA
SCOTT**

Continues the
twelve-book series—
36 Hours—in March 1998
with Book Nine

# PARTNERS IN CRIME

The storm was over, and Detective Jack Stryker finally had a prime suspect in Grand Springs' high-profile murder case. But beautiful Josie Reynolds wasn't about to admit to the crime—nor did Jack want her to. He believed in her innocence, and he teamed up with the alluring suspect to prove it. But was he playing it by the book—or merely blinded by love?

For Jack and Josie and *all* the residents of Grand Springs, Colorado, the storm-induced blackout was just the beginning of 36 Hours that changed *everything!* You won't want to miss a single book.

Available at your favorite retail outlet.

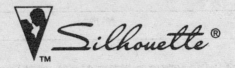

# SILHOUETTE®
## *Desire*®

**M**
*of the*
**A**
*Month*
**N**

*1998*

There is no sexier, stronger, more irresistible hero than Silhouette Desire's *Man of the Month*. And you'll find him steaming up the pages of a sensual and emotional love story written by the bestselling and most beloved authors in the genre.

Just look who's coming your way for the first half of 1998:

| | |
|---|---|
| January #1117 | **THE COWBOY STEALS A LADY** by Anne McAllister |
| February #1123 | **THE BRENNAN BABY** by Barbara Boswell |
| March #1129 | **A BABY IN HIS IN-BOX** by Jennifer Greene |
| April #1135 | **THE SEDUCTION OF FIONA TALLCHIEF** by Cait London *(The Tallchiefs)* |
| May #1141 | **THE PASSIONATE G-MAN** by Dixie Browning *(The Lawless Heirs)* |

**Man of the Month**
only from

# SILHOUETTE® *Desire*®

**You can find us at your favorite retail outlet.**

# THE BABY OF THE MONTH CLUB

*RITA -Award- Winning Author*

# MARIE FERRARELLA's

*miniseries continues with her brand-new Silhouette single title*

# In The Family Way

Dr. Rafe Saldana was Bedford's most popular pediatrician. And though the handsome doctor had a whole lot of love for his tiny patients, his heart wasn't open for business with women. At least, not until single mother Dana Morrow walked into his life. But Dana was about to become the newest member of the Baby of the Month Club. Was the dashing doctor ready to play daddy to her baby-to-be?

Available June 1998.

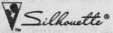

Silhouette®

Find this new title by Marie Ferrarella at your favorite retail outlet.

PSMFIFWAY